SPHERE

Elise Noble

Published by Undercover Publishing Limited

Copyright © 2020 Elise Noble

v3

ISBN: 978-1-912888-22-1

Edited by Nikki Mentges

Cover design by Elise Noble

www.undercover-publishing.com

www.elise-noble.com

Expect the unexpected.
And whenever possible, be the unexpected.

CHAPTER 1

I CHECKED MY phone for the tenth time in as many minutes, willing it to ring. A hostage negotiation, a shoot-out, a sting operation, a last-minute assassination... Anything would have been better than what Bradley had planned for me today.

Speak of the devil. He appeared in my bedroom doorway, bouncing on his toes.

"Are you ready? Why aren't you ready?" He put his hands on his hips. "Emmy, you're still in your pyjamas."

"Technically, these aren't pyjamas."

I always slept in a pair of boxer shorts and an oversized T-shirt, borrowed from my husband's closet. In my world, comfort came before style.

"Stop being facetious and hurry up. Everyone else is ready and raring to go."

Really? When I got into the hallway—now dressed under protest—Ana was sitting on one couch and Dan, Mack, and Carmen were on the other, all looking as if they were waiting to head to the gas chamber rather than take a fun-packed trip to Virginia's newest family attraction. Honestly, I'd seen more enthusiasm amongst prisoners of war, and I couldn't blame the girls. SciPark was billed as "education meets entertainment," but to me, it felt like the fine line between purgatory and full-on hell. Hellgatory. Was that a thing? Only the kids seemed excited—Trick, Vine, Race, Josh, and Tabby—although I suspected Tabby would have been just as happy if Ana had taken her out the back and taught her how to shoot a crossbow. The kid was only three years old, and though I'd never admit it to my sister, Tabby made me very nervous.

"I still don't understand why I have to go," Mack said, clutching her laptop bag like a shield. "None of these children are mine."

Bradley gave an overly theatrical sigh. "You want to be a mother, don't you?"

"Someday."

"Well, think of this as practice."

I raised my hand. "I don't want to be a mother, ever, so can I be excused?"

"No."

"Why not?"

"Somebody needs to stop Ana from murdering Bradley," Dan muttered. "And that somebody is you."

"Remember what happened when he made us go to the spa?" Carmen asked. "We had to dig a grave. I'm not digging another grave, not even Bradley's."

"Fine, I'll come. But I'm not going on any of the bloody rides."

Ana leaned in close. "Why do you let him boss you around like this? You pay his salary, don't you?"

Good question. With an equally excellent answer.

"Because he's watched *FernGully* fifty times in the last fortnight, and he wants to plant a replica rainforest in the backyard."

"A rainforest? How can he? We're in Virginia. It's

too cold."

"He also wants to build a giant greenhouse to go over the top. I caught him researching habitats for marmosets, and there's no way we're getting monkeys. No bloody way. The parakeets around the swimming pool were bad enough, and don't even get me started on the swans. Anyhow, SciPark's got a living rainforest, and I'm hoping that if he realises how badly the humidity will frizz his hair, he'll have a rethink."

"Why don't we all chip in and send him on a trip to Borneo instead?"

"Hmm... That's actually not a bad idea. Guys—"

"Hurry! Hurry!" Bradley clapped his hands together. "If you don't get a move on, there's no point in us going at all."

"I'm not seeing a problem with that."

"Of course, staying here *would* give me more time to work on my biosphere plans..."

"Okay, okay, I'm hurrying."

Finally, we got everyone loaded into three cars. Three cars because if we only took two, then Mack would have had to ride with Dan and she didn't have a death wish. So Dan took Race—her newly adopted son—plus his two buddies, I got Ana and Tabby, and Mack brought up the rear with Carmen and Josh. And Bradley, after he ran back inside to fetch his sunscreen and then again for his sun visor and yet again because his new shoes were rubbing. So much for leaving quickly.

While we were waiting, Ana glanced at her watch and sighed as Carmen tried to work out where to stuff

Bradley's enormous purse.

"I could have gone climbing after all. Sam will be back before we get out of the gates."

Sam Quinn, Ana's significant other, had taken a trip to Seneca Rocks with a group of his CIA buddies. A last-minute invite, so he said, and funnily enough, one that had only materialised after Bradley invited him to join us today. Ditto for Carmen's husband and his sudden desire to audit the camera system at the California office of Blackwood Security, the company he and I co-owned along with my husband and Nick Goldman.

"I'm surprised you agreed to come in the first place," I said.

Ana wasn't a fan of crowds, not unless she was using them as a cover for something nefarious. Then she'd suck it up and deal.

"Bradley plays dirty. He showed Tabby a video of the big wheel, and now she wants to ride on it." Another sigh. "I suppose it'll be educational."

"Let's hope there's a bar."

"You're driving."

"Maybe I'll make Bradley drive back."

"You can't. Sam and I have dinner reservations tomorrow, and if Bradley plays chauffeur, we'll still be somewhere around Fredericksburg."

"Fine, then I'll have to settle for coffee."

Bradley ran out of the house once more, and this time he was wearing sparkly pink hi-tops and matching sunglasses. I was half-surprised he hadn't changed his hair colour as well, but that was still turquoise.

"Can we go now?" I yelled out of the Porsche's window. I'd borrowed my husband's Cayenne. He didn't need it today because when Bradley suggested he might like to tag along, he'd helicoptered to the airfield and flown to Barcelona. Coward. Now the Porsche had a custom-made hot-pink leather baby seat installed in the back—courtesy of Bradley, of course—and I had a good mind to leave it there as a punishment.

"Yes, but if you're going to be snippy, then I'll ride with Mack."

Ana settled back in her seat and adjusted her aviators. "Good. Snippiness rules."

In the rear-view mirror, Tabby mimicked her mother with her own Babiators, and I suppressed a shudder. I loved my niece, don't get me wrong, but... yeah. She wasn't a normal child. Kids scared me, I freely admitted that, but Tabby was a weird cross between a mini mercenary and a toddler, and I was never quite sure how to handle her.

Half of my little group of friends had kids now. I had a feeling Mack would soon join the club as well. That would leave me and Sofia as the only two non-moms, but Sofia had just connected with her long-lost brother, and he lived overseas, so she was travelling quite a bit. Which left me a little...not lonely, exactly, but I felt as if people were moving on without me. We'd always be there for each other, of that I was certain, and of course I was happy that they were happy, but still... Perhaps *that* was the real reason I was going today. I didn't want to get left behind while their lives changed for good.

CHAPTER 2

AT THE PARK'S main gate, a bored-looking teenager in a SciPark baseball cap charged us a fortune, then issued us with paper maps.

"There's an app too," he told us in a monotone speech he'd obviously given a thousand times. "Your Wi-Fi password's printed on your ticket, and the audio tour's available in thirteen different languages."

Thirteen? Couldn't they have added one more to avoid bad luck? If I'd known what was to come, perhaps I'd have taken that as a sign. But since I'd left my crystal ball at home, I trailed into the park oblivious, hanging back as Bradley bounded on ahead in a silver jumpsuit that probably cost me a thousand bucks.

According to the map, the park was laid out in a series of concentric circles, nine of them, kind of like Dante's Inferno except the middle was dominated by a giant silver sphere rather than a lake of ice. There were over six hundred exhibits. No way would we get through everything in one day, but I wasn't about to mention that to Bradley because he'd probably check us into a hotel and then we'd be stuck there forever.

"What do you want to do first, guys?" Dan asked, her question aimed at her three boys. When she adopted ten-year-old Race not so long ago, his two older buddies had come as part of the package. Nobody minded. Before the trio crossed paths with Blackwood, they'd spent most of their time getting into trouble on the streets, the result of parents who just didn't care. Now Trick, the eldest at fifteen, spent most of his spare time hanging out in Dan's boyfriend's recording studio, Vine had recently discovered baseball, and Race—or Caleb if one was to use his actual name, which Dan tended to—liked to come to the office. We'd given him a desk next to Dan's, and he must have had the best grades in school considering the amount of help he got with his homework. They'd turned out to be good kids, even if their morals could be questionable at times. None of us were in a position to judge them for that. So far today, they'd been taking care of Josh, even though he was seven years old and probably ruined their street cred.

Dan was the only one of us who looked vaguely happy to be at SciPark. Probably because the three older boys could fend for themselves, meaning she was ready to hit the non-alcoholic cocktails at ten in the morning. On any other day, Carmen might have been okay with the trip as well, but her new rifle had been delivered yesterday, and I knew what she'd rather be doing.

"Can we see the dinosaurs?" Josh asked, and everyone else shrugged.

Jurassic Park it wasn't. Live dinosaurs would have been an interesting spectacle, but these were all made of plastic and the ones that did move just jerked around on the spot while roars sounded through loudspeakers.

"How do they know what dinosaurs sounded like?" Race asked.

Good question, and I had no idea of the answer. It wasn't something I needed to know in my line of work. Perhaps if I ever had to go undercover as a palaeontologist... Thankfully, Mack and Dr. Google were on the case.

"Okay, so nobody actually does know what dinosaurs sounded like. Scientists just guess based on the shape of their nasal and throat passages." She scrolled down farther on her tablet. "In fact, they think a T-Rex made a low rumble, and birds honked rather than sang."

"Then why don't these pterodactyls honk?"

"Do you know how many guns there are in America?" I asked. "If we had to put up with constant honking, somebody would shoot the things."

"But the sign at the entrance said no guns are allowed inside the park?"

Ah, such innocence. I glanced at Ana, and she smirked back. Dan obviously hadn't corrupted her son completely yet.

"Why don't we move on to the rainforest?"

"Wait, where's Josh?" Carmen reappeared with a bag of donuts, and boy did I need the carbs.

"Bradley took him to the gift shop."

"And you *let* him?"

"I didn't think it would hurt. Neither of them'll want to carry stuff around the park all day."

"You didn't think it would hurt?" Carmen stared daggers at me. "Have you met Bradley?"

Five minutes later, I found myself lugging two bags of assorted shite towards the rainforest as Josh waddled along beside Carmen in his dinosaur costume. Every so often, Carmen gave me a sideways glare, and worse, Race had told Josh about the honking and he'd decided to try it out. And people wondered why I didn't want kids? If this carried on, I might be tempted to use the Walther CCP nestled in the small of my back on myself.

"Isn't this fun?" Bradley asked.

"Do you want an honest answer to that?"

He ignored me completely. "I loooove amusement parks. Next time, we should come for the whole weekend."

Next time, I'd be joining Black in Barcelona. Or perhaps I could fly home to London and visit a few old friends? Bradley could take his chances with Ana. Even the debacle at the health farm had been more fun than this.

Although I had to admit that the rainforest was cooler than I thought it would be, and do you know why? Fake rainforests in Virginia didn't have mosquitos. Or poisonous spiders or bullet ants or giant centipedes. The caterpillars were safely locked up in a glass case, as were the titan beetles, and nobody needed to worry about getting dive-bombed by bees. As with the dinosaur collection, the background noises were piped in, albeit a little more realistic this time.

The long, curved glasshouse took up half of the park's second ring, heated by solar panels that doubled as part of the "Manmade Miracles" exhibit in the next circle. The boys clambered up a wooden staircase to view the "forest" from above while the rest of us meandered along a brick path that wound through the trees below. Having visited the jungle many, many times before, I'd smoothed my hair down with plenty of anti-frizz serum and worn it in a French plait. The other girls had followed suit with sensible styles and plenty of bobby pins. Bradley, on the other hand, looked like the silver-and-turquoise love child of a Q-tip and a cotton candy machine by the time we got to the animal section, and none of us dared to look at each other because we'd have collapsed into giggles.

A girl holding a tame monkey in a lime-green harness seemed to be having a similar reaction. She approached with a smile, but every few seconds, her gaze strayed to Bradley's hair and the corners of her mouth twitched.

"Would you like to meet Jimbo?" she asked. "He's a capuchin monkey. Please don't touch him, though."

"Should he be out with people like that?" Dan asked. "This isn't a circus."

"He only comes out for fifteen minutes twice a day," the girl explained. "The rest of the time, he lives with his friends in the enclosure over there. In an ideal world, the animals here wouldn't be in captivity, but they've all been rescued from bad situations and none of them are suitable for release. Jimbo belonged to a pop star until the guy got sick of having to change his diaper and dumped him at a pseudo-sanctuary."

"A pseudo-sanctuary?"

"One that claims to be a rescue operation, but really they're breeding the animals and selling them. Jimbo's cage hadn't been cleaned for months, and he was just sitting in the corner, rocking. He gets lonely." The girl offered Jimbo a finger, and he held onto it. "See? He seems to identify more with humans than with other monkeys. We tried all sorts of enrichment ideas, but he'd just stand at the bars trying to touch people the whole day. So we're experimenting with outings, and now he seems to be happier."

I guess I understood that. After all, I had a pet jaguar at home. When I first rescued Kitty from a drug lord, I'd consulted various experts, and the final consensus was that he couldn't go back to the Amazon. And also he thought he was a dog. We'd built him a huge cat house at the back of Riverley Hall, but he spent most of his time curled up in the kitchen with my elderly Doberman.

Bradley lined up for a selfie, but the shriek when he activated the front-facing camera on his iPhone made everyone in the glasshouse freeze. Everyone except Jimbo, that was. The monkey jerked the leash out of the keeper's hands, made a grab for Bradley's sunglasses, and ran straight to the nearest tree.

On second thoughts, I preferred the venomous centipedes.

"I'm so sorry!" the keeper gasped. "Jimbo's never done anything like this before."

Of course he hadn't, but he'd also never met Bradley. And I had to hand it to the monkey—he looked good in Gucci.

Bradley made a grab for the leash, missed, then stumbled backwards with his arms windmilling as a caiman leapt towards the glass at the front of its tank and snapped. Jimbo bolted into the upper branches as Bradley landed in something squishy. *Please say that was just mud.* If it was monkey poop, he could get a cab back home.

Carmen snapped a picture, laughing, and Bradley turned on her, all indignant.

"Don't just stand there taking photos! *Do* something."

"What do you want me to do? Shoot it down?"

Everybody within earshot gasped, and Carmen raised her hands.

"I was joking."

I mostly believed that. *Mostly*.

Jimbo leapt to the next tree, swung on a vine Tarzan-style, and landed on the railing of the upper walkway. A group of people who'd been watching the drama unfold screamed and scattered, but not before Jimbo managed to grab a baseball cap and a gold necklace to go with his shades. I was going to hazard a wild guess and say his previous owner had been a rapper rather than a pop star.

The monkey paused long enough to put the chain around his neck, and then he headed for the parakeet enclosure. I'd say he must have lived in a house before because he sure got the door open quickly. A whole flock of parakeets flew out, and I knew from experience how difficult those little bastards were to catch.

A trio of wild-eyed teenagers wearing SciPark polo shirts ran in our direction as the keeper frantically scanned the trees for the bloody monkey. Whoever said never to work with children or animals was absolutely right, and if they'd ever met Bradley, they'd have added him to that list as well.

"We'll have to evacuate the rainforest," one of the rangers said as a parakeet swooped past inches from his head.

Bradley was already halfway to the door. I picked up the bags of shopping, and that's the story of how we got kicked out of the monkey house.

CHAPTER 3

BRADLEY HAD PRACTICALLY brought luggage with him, so while he went to the bathroom to fix his hair and change into fresh clothes because whatever was on his ass didn't smell so good, the rest of us ventured farther into the park. I was strongly considering breaking my "no alcohol" pledge. Surely one gin and tonic this early in the day would be okay?

Fuck, Bradley had turned me into a morning drinker.

"Want the wheel," Tabby announced. At three years old, she had the determination to rival most teenagers, but her manners were sadly lacking. "Bradley said wheel."

Mack had downloaded the app by that point—with her being Blackwood's number-one IT geek, I'd have expected nothing less—and while the rest of us were experiencing nature's wonders in the pseudo-rainforest, she'd been busy scrolling through the features.

"Y'all, the top-rated restaurant in this place is right next to the wheel, and according to the blurb, it has a terrace and a cocktail menu."

I crouched down in front of my niece. "Going on the wheel's a great idea, sweetie. Your mama can't wait to take you."

"Mom, can I go on the wheel too?" Josh asked.

Carmen smiled at him. "Of course you can. Ana would love it if you went with her."

Ana's jaw clenched, but she wouldn't turn down a kid.

"I'll buy you a cocktail," Carmen promised Ana.

"This might not be so bad," I said. "The wheel's almost in the centre of the park. If we start there with alcohol, by the end of the afternoon, we'll be sober and also near the cars for a quick getaway."

The other girls nodded their agreement, and Mack pointed us in the right direction. Not that we needed much help. The centrepiece of the park was impossible to miss, the towering silver globe designed by some fancy architect I'd never heard of. They'd named it "Inside Out." On the outside, it was the earth, and on the inside, it was space. If you queued up for long enough, you could traipse through a tunnel billed as a wormhole and ride a gravity-powered roller coaster that took you on a tour of the Milky Way.

"We can do this, people." Dan checked her watch as the kids got distracted by a giant model of a human being. According to the signs, you were meant to walk into it through the mouth, and I dreaded to think where you came out. "Only six more hours to go."

Six more hours... I guess it could have been worse. I could have been staking out a Taliban stronghold, or trekking across Siberia, or skulking around a secure facility with armed guards at every turn. Or shopping. This was better than shopping.

The staff at the Steampunk Saloon welcomed us with open arms and bar snacks. Dan's boys headed for the space sphere, where the line snaked out the door at the bottom and wound through the surrounding grassy park. A handful of groups had already set out picnic blankets, chairs, and even an inflatable sunlounger, although I couldn't see them staying there for long if the black clouds on the horizon crept much closer. Ana headed towards the Ferris wheel with Tabby and Josh, and thankfully the line for that was much shorter. On a scale of bad to terrible, I figured her mood would rate as "foul" by the time we left at the end of the day.

The drinks menu contained a variety of mixological delights. Dan ordered a Steam Engine, Mack picked a Clockwork Orange, and Carmen decided on a Molecular Marvel.

"And for you?" the waitress asked me.

"Two Death in the Afternoons. Or should that be Deaths in the Afternoon?"

She giggled. "Two? Are you sure? Those have absinthe in them."

"One's for my friend. And could you bring a few bags of chips?"

A blur of turquoise streaking across the plaza below caught my eye. Good grief. Bradley had tamed his hair, but now he'd found a matching jumpsuit and he looked like a speeding crayon. Somehow, he managed to spot Ana in a sea of hundreds and made a beeline straight for her, squeezing under the barrier near the front of the line. Josh unhooked Bradley's manbag when it snagged on the railing.

"Uh, excuse me?" I waved the waitress back over. "Would you mind making that three Deaths?"

Ana wasn't driving, and she'd sure as hell need the drinks. At least the gondolas were enclosed glass. I'd have feared for Bradley's safety otherwise. When they climbed on board, he was yack-yack-yacking and Ana's expression was blacker than the ever-nearing storm clouds. Hmm. If it started raining, would Bradley let us go home early?

The bar was nearly empty at that time of day, and our drinks arrived quickly. Mack already had her laptop out, and Carmen was texting someone. Probably Nate. Dan sipped her Steam Engine while she watched the boys edging closer to the sphere. Race in particular, judging by the quiet smile on her lips.

"Enjoying motherhood?" I asked softly.

After a moment, she nodded. "Still getting used to it, but yes."

"Guess it'll take a while. Three months ago, your whole life got turned upside down. The non-Blackwood parts, at least."

"Tell me about it. I used to have a routine—get home, change, go out for dinner, hit a club. Now I have to *make* dinner."

"How's that working out?"

"I understand why Mack's on first-name terms with most of the fire department."

"Is Race settling in okay?"

"I think so. We're all still getting to know each other. I wish I'd been around for his early years, but I can't turn back the clock."

"At least you missed the terrible twos."

"I suppose that's a blessing."

"Ethan seems smitten. With both of you."

Dan actually blushed, which was a first. But she'd changed a lot since she started dating Ethan White. "He's everything I always thought I'd never have."

I squeezed her hand. "I'm glad you're happy."

"I—"

"*¡Caramba!*" Carmen burst out laughing. "The wheel has stopped."

"Isn't that a good thing?" Dan asked. "Ana can get off now."

"No, I mean it's *stopped*, stopped. Kaput. It jolted then shuddered to a halt, and now the rangers are looking confused."

"Where's Ana?"

We all turned to look. Ah, shit. They were on the right at roughly three o'clock. Ana and Tabby, a baby T-Rex, and a human peacock. Bradley's jumpsuit was a beacon of bad taste on an otherwise grey day.

Mack held an imaginary phone up to her ear. "911? I'd like to report a murder."

"It's not funny," I chided. But it was. Mack got the giggles, and as soon as I looked at Dan, we both started laughing too, and none of us could stop.

"Uh, is everything okay?" the waitress asked.

"Do me a favour and bring another Death?"

"But your friend hasn't drunk the first two?"

"No, but she's trapped on the wheel. Trust me, she'll drink them when she gets off."

The waitress peered past us. "It's stuck?"

"Seems that way."

"It must be those darn monkeys."

"Monkeys?" Like, plural?

"I heard a monkey escaped in the living rainforest, and then he let his friends out. One of them got into the mechanical room and started pulling out wires."

Oops. Good thing Ana wasn't aware of that little tidbit of information.

"Have they caught the monkeys yet?"

"Not yet, but all the spare rangers have been called over to help." The waitress pasted on a bright smile. "I'm sure it'll be sorted out in a jiffy. SciPark never normally has problems like this."

"Perhaps I *should* have shot Jimbo when I had the chance," Carmen muttered as the waitress hurried off.

Sometimes, I worried that Carmen was a little too trigger-happy.

"You mean with a dart gun, right?"

"Of course."

Because I couldn't resist, I picked up the phone and dialled Ana. "Having fun?"

"*Idi nahui, suka.*"

"I've ordered you a drink."

"I don't need a drink, I need a roll of duct tape."

"Why don't we all try meditating?" Bradley asked in the background. "I have an app on my phone."

"Is the duct tape for you or for Bradley?"

"Find out what's going on. *Please.*"

It wasn't like Ana to beg, but since she was stranded in a closet-sized space with three children, I could kind of understand why she'd slipped out of character. Although she was an excellent assassin, the best, her upbringing had been unconventional to say the least, and as a result, she didn't do so well in social situations. Chatter drove her crazy.

"Guys, I'm gonna try and find out how long the power outage is likely to last."

"Want some company?" Dan offered.

"Why not?"

Now that Mack had her laptop open, she showed no signs of wanting to leave it, but she did give us the briefest of smirks.

"I'll have a snoop around electronically. SciPark has three private Wi-Fi networks as well as the guest one. I'll bet there are emails flying around."

I raised an eyebrow in Carmen's direction, and she raised her glass.

"We shouldn't let the drinks go to waste. How about I call you if the wheel starts working again?" She focused over my shoulder. "Looks as if the sphere has a glitch too."

Dan and I turned in time to see a man placing a temporary barrier in front of the doors. The waiting crowd didn't seem happy, but they began to move backwards.

"Did the boys already go in?" I asked.

"Just a minute ago," Dan said.

"Let's hope they're not hanging upside down on a roller coaster, eh?"

"Ah, shit. I'd better call Caleb." A pause. "No answer."

"Does the roller coaster have lap bars or one of those restraint systems that goes over your shoulders? If he's on board and strapped down, he might not be able to reach his phone."

Of course, with Dan being Dan and second in command at Blackwood's investigations division, she checked. A quick Google search showed that Inside Out did indeed have bulky over-the-shoulder restraints. Safety first. Then again, it also had a height restriction and I was pretty sure Race must have stood on tiptoes to get around that.

"I guess that's possible," she admitted.

"Or perhaps the ride's still going and he's having fun? Phoning Mom probably isn't top of his list of things to do. Why don't you send him a text?"

"Just did."

I spotted a ranger scurrying in the direction of the rainforest and jogged after him. He clearly didn't appreciate being stopped, but he also wasn't openly rude, so I forced a smile.

"Any idea what's going on with the wheel?"

"It's stuck."

No kidding. "Is there an ETA on it getting unstuck? I've got friends on board."

"Probably a while. We've been told to catch the monkeys and the parakeets first."

"What about the Inside Out ride?" Dan asked.

"The supervisor radioed to say there's been a power failure. He said they've closed it down."

The aforementioned radio on the ranger's belt bleeped, and a panicked voice crackled through.

"One of the monkeys let the capybaras out. Lorinda saw them running towards the lake."

Capybaras? I didn't know much about those, but the ranger broke into a jog. We were on our own again. Would they close the park? As far as I knew, there weren't any *really* dangerous animals here—only Bradley's nemesis the caiman, plus a few snakes—but this was fast descending into chaos. One time, just *one* time, couldn't we have a day out without drama?

Dan's phone rang, and she checked the screen before she pressed it to her ear. "Caleb," she mouthed.

Well, that was one small piece of good news.

Or was it?

As Dan listened, the colour drained out of her face, and I began to get a bad, bad feeling in my gut. Dan had trekked through the jungle to start a war with a drug-peddling psychopath with barely a hint of nerves. She chased terrorists for fun.

"Hide." She listened a moment. "No, no, no! Promise me you'll hide. We're on our way. Love you, okay?"

On our way to do what?

Suddenly, being stuck on the wheel with Bradley was beginning to look like the more attractive option.

CHAPTER 4

"WHAT'S WRONG?" I asked the instant Dan hung up.

"There's a man with a gun inside the sphere, and he's taken everyone on the ride hostage. Fuck, I feel sick."

Oh. Fuck indeed.

I was already evaluating. The sphere was closed, cordoned off due to a technical fault. Was there genuinely an electrical or mechanical problem? Or was that a ruse? If it was the latter, that suggested at least some degree of organisation rather than a total nutter acting on impulse. Plus he'd managed to sneak a gun past security. Sure, we'd all managed it too, but we'd also had plenty of practice at that sort of thing. Who were we up against?

And more to the point, how the hell were we meant to get inside the oversized ball bearing? Apart from the entrance at the front—now closed—I couldn't even see a door.

"What else did Race say?"

"Not much. I didn't want him talking. The train pulled up to the empty platform, and the man was there waiting. Race was sitting at the back with Vine, and he managed to wriggle out of his restraints and crawl back along the track, but everyone else is stuck in the cars. Last thing Race heard, the fucker was demanding everyone's phones."

"Any idea what the guy wants?"

"No clue. We've got to get in there."

This was as shaken as I'd ever seen Dan, and considering she'd nearly been burned to a crisp by a madman earlier in the year, that was saying something.

"And we *will* get in there, but we'll do it the right way. We've spent half our lives training for this shit. It's one guy and a roller coaster. A walk in the park."

Quite literally, and as we hustled back across the plaza to the Steampunk Saloon, I called Ana with an update. I was in two minds about developments. Yes, I'd been bored out of my skull, but did I really want to get into another gunfight?

"Hey, *suka*. So there's a teeny problem."

"They can't find an engineer? Everyone just ran off to the east side of the park, and Bradley won't stop singing."

In the background, I heard three voices mullering one of the songs from *Frozen*, and when I looked up at the pod on the right-hand side of the wheel, Ana was sitting on the floor at one end with her knees drawn up to her chest and her hands over her ears. I took her foul mood and raised it to heinous.

"They're probably chasing the capybaras."

"The what?"

"Never mind. We've got bigger things to worry about—apparently there's a hostage situation in the giant silver sphere. Can you see any unusual activity from up there? A guy came out and closed it ten minutes ago, but I wasn't paying much attention after that."

Now Ana got to her feet, and her assessment took

seconds. We'd both done it a thousand times, looked over a scene a regular person wouldn't blink twice at and identified areas of concern. People out of place, objects where they shouldn't be, counter-surveillance, possible dangers.

"Nothing's happening. Doors are locked. A teenager just tried them, but now he's walking away. There's a notice pinned to the outside. What kind of a hostage situation?"

"Not sure at the moment. Race got away, but he couldn't talk much. One guy with a gun that he saw, but maybe more."

"Is he in danger?"

"Depends whether they realise he's missing or not." Dan stiffened beside me. "Can you see any other doors?"

"Not on this side."

"Keep watching, okay? We need to get gear from the cars."

And brief Mack and Carmen. And keep Dan calm. And come up with a coherent plan, all while avoiding packs of marauding wildlife. No biggie.

Mack and Carmen were relaxing with their drinks and a platter of nibbles when we jogged up the outside stairs to the terrace. Thankfully there was only one other occupied table, and that was in the far corner. I did *not* want to be having this conversation with an audience.

"A bunch of capybaras escaped," Mack told us. "Did you know they can run as fast as a small horse, and if they get into water, they can stay under for five minutes?"

"We heard, but there's a more pressing matter right

now." I took the cocktail out of her hand. "You need to put that down."

Her smile faded. "Why? What's going on?"

I gave her a brief overview. "Can you find us any more info? I know damn well you can't spend more than five minutes in front of a computer without attempting *something* illegal. Are you in their network?"

"Just the outer fringes. But the security was set up by a first-grader, so it shouldn't take long. Can you believe their Wi-Fi passwords are only six characters long?"

"We need camera feeds. And we also need to find a way inside the sphere. Look for staff maps, floor plans, anything. And find out who the supervisors are. One of them informed the rangers there'd been a power failure over there, and we're not sure if that genuinely happened, or whether he was forced to say it, or if he was even involved somehow."

"What if the power failure at the wheel was a distraction?" Dan asked, and I was pleased she'd got her head back into the game. "The monkeys would make a convenient scapegoat."

"Anything's possible. But we can do the post-mortem later. Let's get our kit."

A scream from below made me swivel in a heartbeat. A quick scan of the plaza around the sphere didn't reveal the source, but then Carmen elbowed me in the side.

"*¡Qué hostia!* She's insane."

Now what? When I turned, I saw Ana had pried open the hatch on the glass pod she was in, and now she was halfway along one arm of the wheel with her arms stretched out to the sides like a high-wire artiste. Bloody hell.

"Can't disagree with you there."

Bradley was busy sealing the pod with what looked like neon-pink washi tape while Josh and Tabby sat on the bench seat. Bradley may have been a lunatic, but in a situation like this one, he'd step up to the plate. And I was glad Ana would have my back when we went into the sphere. We connected. I knew how she'd react in any given situation and vice versa. If I couldn't have Black by my side, then Ana made a worthy substitute.

Gasps came from below as she slid down a vertical support pointing to six o'clock as if it were a fireman's pole, and she neatly sidestepped when a ranger tried to speak to her. Moments later, she disappeared into the milling crowd. Nicely done.

Of course, she didn't come in our direction. No, she'd drawn too much attention to herself and we didn't need any extra scrutiny, not with what we were about to do. The lack of activity around the sphere suggested nobody except us had realised what was going on in there. That gave me hope that we could do a quick smash-and-dash. Get in, get our kids, get the hell out of there, then leave the cops to clear up the aftermath.

Dan's phone rang.

She already had it in her hand, and I caught a glimpse of the name on the screen. Vine was calling. Dan didn't put him on speaker for obvious reasons, but I squashed in close enough to hear.

"Vine?" she whispered. "You okay?"

He didn't answer, but we did hear another voice in the background. Male but shrill. Agitated.

"Shut up. Shut up! Everybody shut up and we won't need to hurt anyone."

Smart kid. Vine, who was suspiciously proficient at being sneaky and also had enough guts to disobey the kidnappers, had managed to open a line so we could hear what was going on. Had he used his smartwatch? Dan had gifted it to him for his birthday last month so he could listen to audiobooks—his dyslexia meant reading was a chore rather than a pleasure for him, and she didn't want him to miss out—and I suspected the investment had just paid off big time. We'd have ears for as long as his battery lasted.

"Keep your hands where we can see them! In the air. Higher!"

That was the second time the unsub—the unknown subject—had referred to "we." There was an outside chance he was bluffing, but for now, we had to assume we'd be dealing with more than one person when we got inside. And if this guy's demeanour was anything to go by, they'd be nervous and slightly unstable.

"Stay here and listen," I told Dan. "I'll take Carmen with me. Plus if you can, have a mooch around the sphere while you're waiting. See if you can spot another door."

"What if Caleb tries to call again?"

"I'll text him and tell him to call me instead, and if he does, Carmen can phone Mack with any news. Once we get back, we'll have proper comms gear. Mack, can you get onto the research team and find out who owns this place? If we've got hostages, then I'd expect some sort of demand. Money is the obvious one, but they may have a different objective. We need to know what it is."

"I'll call Luke."

"I thought he was sick? Practically on his deathbed, you said."

"Uh..."

"You fibbed?"

Mack raised a finger to her lips. "Don't tell Bradley, okay?"

I just rolled my eyes and set off for the car park.

Black had been drilling the importance of being prepared into me for sixteen years, and good little Girl Scout that I was, I'd brought enough gear to start a small war and finish it too. Ana had done the same, and Carmen's trunk resembled a sporting goods store. Dan's kit wasn't quite so useful today, but if you ever needed to do a forensic investigation, she was your girl. Ana was already packing goodies into a slim black backpack when we arrived.

"Claustrophobia got to you?" I asked.

"I don't do singalongs."

That was probably for the best. Dan could hold a tune, but for the rest of us a karaoke session would breach the Geneva Conventions.

We loaded up with what we needed, fitted covert earpieces and linked to Mack via the headset she was already wearing, then trekked back to the park. We'd got our hands stamped for re-entry on the way out, but Sod's Law dictated we got checked by the jobsworth who wanted to search our bags again before we went back in.

"It's park policy," he said, attempting to stare me down.

Amateur. I locked my gaze onto his until he took a step back, then I glanced over his shoulder.

"Is that a monkey?"

He whirled around. "Where?"

"In that tree over there. Looks as if it's wearing some sort of harness. A green one. Is it supposed to be running around like that?"

Just as I'd hoped, he forgot all about the bags and got on the radio, calling for reinforcements. Super—the fewer people near the sphere, the better. Wherever Jimbo was, I liked to think he was enjoying himself.

I was jogging past a life-size T-Rex when my phone buzzed with an incoming call. Race's name flashed up on the screen, and my heart lurched. We couldn't afford to fuck this up, not for his sake or for Dan's. I'd been there when she lost her first son, and burying another child would break her.

"It's Emmy. You okay?"

"There're two of them on the platform," he whispered. "They've both got guns."

"Where are you? Dan told you to hide."

"I did, but then I snuck back to look."

"Stay the hell out of sight."

"I am."

That kid... When you first met him, he came across as quiet, even timid, but he had more courage than most grown men. And he felt no fucking fear. Secretly, I thought Dan was going to have her hands full in a couple of years because Race wasn't a boy who shied away from trouble.

"Did you hear them say anything?"

"The older guy was talking to someone at the front of the train, but I couldn't hear the words. Are you coming? Is Mom there?"

Sweet how quickly he'd started calling Dan that.

"I've got my stuff, and I'm on my way back. Your mom's trying to find a way in. They've locked the main door, but don't worry—that won't stop us."

One of Blackwood's jobs was penetration testing of major US installations, including the White House. I'd managed to sneak past security twice last year. The sphere wouldn't be a problem.

"Okay."

"Go and hide now."

Race hung up, and I knew he'd do whatever he damn well wanted. Brilliant.

CHAPTER 5

"THE FRONT ENTRANCE is a no-go," Dan told us when we got back to the Steampunk Saloon. "The doors are solid, and people keep walking up to them to read the sign."

"What does it say?" I asked.

"That there's a temporary closure due to a power outage."

Mack glanced up from her laptop. "The power's down, all right. The cameras inside aren't working, and the control room's gone dark. SciPark has an internal message board, and a guy called Jeffrey Monteith posted to say he's evacuated the riders and stayed to keep an eye on the place. According to the staff directory, he's a supervisor."

"Interesting."

"You know what else is interesting? The directory also lists a Kelbyn Monteith. He's a ranger in the space sector." She angled the screen towards me. "See?"

Oh, I saw. I saw the same wavy brown hair, the same slightly protruding eyes, the same narrow jaw. Jeffrey looked to be in his late forties, and I put Kelbyn at twenty-two or twenty-three. The family resemblance was all too obvious. What were the chances that father and son were in this together?

"Find out everything you can about them."

"Luke's already doing that." She pressed a few keys. "We've got a better recording of him. Listen."

The voice came through my earpiece, and the unsub still sounded nervous. Edgy. "Why is this seat empty?"

"The kid sitting there got scared just before the ride started," Vine told him. "He ran back outside."

"Check the wormhole," the man ordered an accomplice. "Make sure he left."

"Ah, fuck," I muttered.

"It's okay," Dan told me. "Caleb's hiding, and he's good at that."

"It's not okay. He called me, and he's moving around in there. I told him to stay hidden, but..."

Fear flickered in Dan's eyes. "We need to get in. I found another door on the far side of the sphere, but it's got no handles on the outside. Looks like a fire exit. There's also a moveable camera on a pole near the snack kiosk over there." She pointed to a small building shaped like a flying saucer. "It points towards the rear door."

"Is the camera manual or automatic?"

"On a timer, I think. The motion arc covers the door, but the camera sweeps back and forth at regular intervals. There are two points where the door's invisible to the all-seeing eye—the shortest gap is only five seconds, but the longest gives us twenty-seven seconds to open the door and get inside between passes."

Less than half a minute? Great. Plus we'd need to avoid arousing the suspicions of the employees at the kiosk or any punters who happened to be hanging around.

"Can you stop the feed?" I asked Mack.

"Still working on it. Whoever set up the security cameras used a different password, and that one isn't so easy to crack."

"Guess we'd better keep our fingers crossed for the monkeys, eh?"

"There might be a way to lever the door open," Ana said. "The mechanism on the pod thing was easy to bypass."

"So let's take a look."

The Steampunk Saloon was getting busier, but a few drops of rain had encouraged people to eat indoors, leaving Mack in relative solitude as she huddled under a huge umbrella outside. We borrowed the bathroom to change our jackets and stash extra weapons about our persons, and a quick rummage through Bradley's bags of crap revealed a bunch of scarves we could use to cover our faces. The only downside? They were multicoloured and decorated with dinosaur silhouettes. I picked out the T-Rex and passed Ana the velociraptor. It seemed appropriate.

Mack had patched Vine's device into the comms system, and every so often, we heard another demand to stay still or be quiet. The remainder of the speech was too garbled or too far away to make out, although the hum of voices in the background told us people were talking.

The few drops of rain turned into a steady drizzle as Dan, Ana, Carmen, and I crossed the plaza towards the sphere, the four of us hurrying as if we were looking for shelter. Unfortunately, a bunch of other people had come up with the same idea, and where the sphere bulged outwards, they'd huddled beneath the overhang.

"I hate having an audience," Ana muttered.

"You and me both."

But the situation was what it was, and we had to make the best of it.

Over the years, we'd all learned enough about security cameras to understand their fields of view. We stood just out of range, pretending to discuss where to go next as we waited for the right moment.

"Now," I said, and Mack started a countdown.

We moved as one to the rear entrance, which was barely visible against the silver skin of the sphere. Whoever designed the place had made the door curved, almost seamless. Even the hinges were hidden. The rest of us shielded Ana as she probed for a weak point, somewhere she could insert the blade of a knife.

"Anything?" I asked.

"Nothing yet."

"Ten seconds," Mack reminded us.

With my team and several escaped monkeys as witnesses, I was never visiting an amusement park again.

"Prepare to move away," I ordered, but the faintest scrape from inside made me pause.

I checked the angles again. If I flattened myself against the wall, my gut told me the camera should miss me by a whisker. Hopefully. It would be damn close.

"I'm staying. Get back."

Nobody asked questions. We'd worked together for long enough that the others knew I wouldn't make a decision like that without a damn good reason. I tried to look casual while I did my best impression of a dolophones spider. One of those creepy little suckers had wrapped itself around my arm when I was working surveillance in Australia not so long ago, and I'd had to lie there and let it when what I really wanted to do was flick it over to New Zealand. My lovely colleague Mimi had just chuckled under her breath and pointed out the huntsman spider in the tree opposite. Thankfully, I hadn't heard of any arachnids escaping at SciPark yet.

Another scuff from inside. Somebody was definitely on the other side of the door, but who? Friend or foe?

No racing pulse for me, just the tiniest hit of adrenaline, enough to keep me focused as a clunk made the door vibrate. Our mystery person had pushed down on the exit bar. The door swung outwards, slowly, slowly, and I watched the arc of the camera. The five-second gap was coming right up.

I watched.

Waited.

Burst through the opening the instant the camera got out of range, then yanked the door shut behind me. The pitch-black robbed me of one of my senses, but four was enough. Five if you counted the instincts I'd spent the best part of two decades honing. I forced my opponent to the floor, found his shoulders, worked my way to his hands and twisted them behind his back. That took me a second, two at most, and he hadn't yet got around to screaming. I replaced one of my hands with a knee and clamped the free hand over his mouth.

"Shhh."

He complied and went limp.

Hmm. He was kind of small. And he smelled vaguely of Dan's favourite perfume.

Ah, shit. I loosened my hand.

"Race?"

"I found you a door," he whispered.

At that moment, I knew Race would end up working for Blackwood one day whether Dan liked it or not. I rolled off him and checked him over by feel. He seemed intact.

"Are you hurt?"

"Nah, I'm tough."

I got to my feet, but as I pulled Race up, my spidey senses tingled. We weren't alone. I put a hand over his mouth again, gently this time, a signal rather than a threat. He nodded, and I tucked him behind me.

A narrow flashlight beam played over the wall to my left. Amateur. That made the owner a sitting duck. But so were we. The passage curved to the left, but a few more seconds and whoever it was would be on top of us. The light flashed again, catching the edge of a slim metal cabinet. A yellow zigzag graced the front along with a warning: Danger of Death. No fucking kidding. There was nowhere to hide. Nowhere for us to go but outside, and we couldn't do that. Not only would it be a pain in the ass to get back in again, but if whoever was coming was as unhinged as unsub number one sounded, then I wouldn't put it past him to panic. And gunshots in the plaza weren't something I wanted to contemplate.

Nor did I want to start shooting in the sphere myself. It could be a stray member of the public ahead, or an escaped hostage, and if it wasn't, I didn't want to alert anyone on the platform to my presence by making a noise.

Fortunately, I had the perfect bit of kit with me. I slipped my Fenix PD35 out of my jacket pocket and held it above my head in my left hand, and when our new friend rounded the bend, I hit him with a thousand lumens. In near darkness, the burst of light would be like an explosion behind his eyeballs, and it disoriented him for a couple of seconds—plenty of time for me to close the distance, twist the semi-automatic out of his hand, and dump him on his ass.

Score one point to Blackwood. I cuffed his wrists and tightened two interlinked zip ties just above his knees, allowing him enough movement to shuffle but not to run. Race, bless him, pulled off one of his socks and stuffed it into the asshole's mouth. I hoped it was nice and sweaty.

Time to let the others in.

"Guys? One down, and Race is safe. Let me know when to open the door."

"Fifteen seconds," Dan said, the relief evident in her voice.

"Race, can you open the door for your mom when I tell you?"

He nodded. By then, I'd turned the flashlight onto its economy setting, and I took a moment to study our captive. He'd cut his hair, but there was no doubt about his identity.

"Hi, Kelbyn." His eyes widened at the mention of his name. "Didn't your parents ever tell you not to play with guns?"

"Three... Two... One..." Dan said in my ear, and I half turned to Race.

"Now."

Light flooded in from outside, but only for a moment. Then the whole team was beside me. Dan hugged Race while Ana moved a little way along the passage to watch our six.

"Are you okay?" Dan asked. "Did anybody hurt

you?"

"Nah, they didn't see me. I don't think they're all that smart."

Race may have been young, but he'd already faced more shit on the streets than most people would see in a lifetime. I trusted his judgement. And if the bad guys were dumb, that was both a good thing and a bad thing. Good because we could out-think them. Bad because stupid people were unpredictable.

I took out a gun of my own. With a family day out having turned into a rescue mission, I'd relegated my CCP to an ankle holster as my backup piece—thank goodness Bradley had laid out looser-fitting trousers for me to wear today—and tucked my new Walther PPQ into a shoulder holster under my jacket. Now I cocked it and pointed it at Kelbyn's head.

"We've lost Vine's feed," Mack told me. "Possibly due to battery issues."

There wasn't much I could do about that right now, but it did underscore the urgency of the situation.

"Make a peep without permission, and the next sound you hear will be your brains splattering against the wall." A physical impossibility with his auditory cortex missing, but it scared him nicely. "Nod if you understand."

He nodded.

"Good. I'm going to ask you some questions, and I want brief, honest answers. If I don't get those, it's going to hurt. Got it?"

Another nod. I fished Race's sock out of Kelbyn's mouth. So far, this was going quite well, monkey business excepted. In fact, it was more fun than the actual park.

"You've taken a roller coaster full of people hostage, correct?"

"Y-y-yes."

"Just one group?"

"Yes."

"How many people are you working with?"

"T-t-two."

"Your father's one of them? Jeffrey Monteith?"

"How did you know?"

I applied just a tiny bit of pressure to his windpipe. "I'm asking the questions, not you."

"Yes. Yes!"

The faint smell of urine drifted on the air. Good grief, I'd barely touched him.

"Who else?"

"N-N-Neil Robinson. He works on the ride."

"Are they both on the platform?"

"Neil was in the control booth at the back."

"How do we get there?"

"You won't hurt them, will you?"

"Did we hurt you?"

"Y-y-yes."

"Oh, for goodness' sake. If you think that's pain, you've led a very sheltered life." My words didn't seem to comfort him. "Look, if they cooperate, we'll just secure them and turn them over to the authorities. How do we get to the train?"

Kelbyn deflated a little. Hadn't he realised arrest was inevitable? Nobody got away with holding hostages in the middle of a busy theme park, not unless they were a hell of a lot better prepared, anyway.

"If you follow this hallway and go up the stairs, it brings you out at the far end of the platform."

"I came along the track," Race said. "It's basically a ladder. There's a door on the right, like, twenty yards along."

Good. We could split up. Two on the track and one on the stairs. Somebody needed to stay with Kelbyn and Race, and I was inclined to give that job to Carmen. She was a superb shot, but I wanted to avoid gunfire if at all possible, and Dan was sneakier. She could take the passage, Ana could take Race's route, and I'd go the other way around the track to flank our two targets.

"How does a person get into the booth?" I asked.

Kelbyn looked more miserable than anyone I'd ever seen. "There's a door."

"Which end?"

He had to think about that for a moment. "This side. Facing away from the wormhole. Uh, the main entrance."

"Any steps?"

"Two? Three, maybe?"

"*Why* did you take those people hostage?" Dan asked. "I mean, it's a hell of a risk."

Good question. Sometimes, I tended to get caught up in the nuts and bolts of the operation, but understanding our opponents' motivations could help us.

"We n-n-need drugs."

"Drugs?"

"Y-y-yes."

If they were junkies, that could certainly explain the lack of competence. "And who were you expecting to pay for these drugs?"

Surprisingly, it was Race who answered.

"Artemis and Isolde Sacker. Is that right?"

Kelbyn nodded.

"Who the hell are Artemis and Isolde Sacker?" I asked.

"They're on Instagram." And I wasn't, which probably explained why I'd never heard of them. "We were talking to them in the line." Race stood on tiptoe to whisper in Dan's ear, but because she was wearing an earpiece, I heard every word. "Trick likes Isolde, and Vine kept teasing him, so Trick made us sit at the back while he sat at the front with her."

"Mack, are you getting this?" I asked softly.

"Sure am. Artemis and Isolde are Instagram influencers. Three million and two-point-five million followers respectively. They've both made posts about their visit to SciPark today, which means they were probably gifted free tickets, but they mostly seem to focus on make-up. Seems they've recently started their own brand. It's called Artis. Hey, the lip gloss is on special offer."

"So you're expecting the hostages to pay their own ransoms?" Dan asked. "That's new."

"No, th-th-their father," Kelbyn said. "We were going to call him."

"This was a spur-of-the-moment thing? You just saw the Sacker girls walk into the park this morning and thought you could make a few bucks?"

"We found out yesterday that they were c-c-coming. They were on the VIP list."

I had one more question before we headed up to the platform. "Are your cohorts armed?"

"They both have pistols."

Oh, fantastic. More guns. But on balance, walking into the line of fire was still better than visiting the gift shop with Bradley.

Chapter 6

WE TURNED OFF the flashlights and moved by feel as we ventured deeper into the bowels of the sphere. It was slow going. We couldn't afford to make any noise, and in the gloom, it would be all too easy to bump into something accidentally.

Race's estimate of twenty yards to the door was spot on, and I felt rather than saw Ana smile in the darkness before we went our separate ways. I'd definitely drawn the short straw. Not only did I have the farthest to go, but my section of track rose almost vertically at times. A kidnapping at a freaking amusement park... In some ways, it wasn't a *terrible* plan. I mean, the hostages had literally climbed onto the roller coaster and incapacitated themselves. And by having staff members involved, they could maintain a cover-up, at least for a short period of time. They'd gotten lucky with Jimbo's escape, but I suspected Dan might be right about the busted Ferris wheel being intentional. If I'd needed to plan a distraction, that's how I'd have played it. Distressed passengers in full view of everyone but no real danger.

The execution of the rest, however? Poor. One out of ten, two if I was feeling generous.

"The Sacker family's mega-rich. I'm sending a picture," Mack told us. I shielded the glow from my phone screen as a photo of two Barbie dolls popped up. "Artemis is eighteen years old, and Isolde's fifteen. The girls' father is the CEO of Bio-D Pharmaceuticals and, by all accounts, a bit of a slimeball. If Martin Shkreli is Pharma Bro, then David Sacker's his daddy."

When Mack said that, I realised I knew the man already.

"David Sacker? I've met him."

Once upon a time, he'd hit up my husband to invest in one of his projects. But despite being an assassin, Black still had some morals. For him to invest in a biotech company, it had to adhere to a set of principles, which meant treating staff like shit and price-gouging were both big no-nos. Bio-D met absolutely none of his criteria. Plus Sacker referred to me as "your little lady," so Black had told him to fuck off, albeit slightly more politely than that.

"Are the stories true?" Mack asked.

"Is it wrong to be rooting for the kidnappers?"

A faint glow from the tunnel ahead let me see the track properly for the first time. Emergency lighting from the platform? I suspected so, and that meant I was getting close.

"Almost there," Ana whispered.

A few moments passed, and then Dan spoke, her words so quiet they were barely audible. "I got right up to the platform. Jeffrey's getting agitated, I think because he can't raise Kelbyn."

"Any sign of contestant number three?" I asked.

"Not yet. The door of the booth is open a crack, and there's dim light inside, but no movement."

"I'm not far away. When I get there, let's—"

"Uh-oh."

What was the problem? I strained my ears and heard a man's voice in the background. "...go and find him."

"The good news is that Robinson's left the booth," Ana told me.

The bad news? He'd presumably gone down the passageway and was heading right for Dan. Fuck it. I abandoned my chimp-like traverse of the roller-coaster track and ran across the rungs instead. Either I'd get there faster or I'd break my ankle.

Wish me luck.

The sounds of a scuffle came over the radio as I burst onto the platform. Jeffrey Monteith was striding towards the passage, and I sprinted in his direction. Too late, he heard me coming, and as I rugby-tackled him, Ana grabbed the gun out of his hand, popped the magazine, and sent both parts skidding across onto the track. They dropped down the side of the train with a metallic clatter.

Jeffrey wriggled like a demented caterpillar, but with me sitting on his legs and Ana hanging onto his arms, he couldn't do much more than yell. Then Ana stuffed a ball gag into his mouth—a fucking ball gag— and he shut up.

"Okay?" she asked.

"Yup."

A moment later, she was gone, looking into the control booth in case Kelbyn had lied about the number of assholes.

"Clear."

"Check the other corridor? The one that goes to the front entrance?"

"*Da.*"

I glanced briefly at the train and saw a few dropped jaws. "Everybody stay quiet, got it?"

Where was Dan? Back in the day, we'd gleefully waded into bar brawls every other weekend, so I knew she was perfectly capable of taking care of herself, but she didn't get into so many fights nowadays. Car crashes, sure, but not punch-ups.

Still, I needn't have worried. Twenty seconds later, she marched Neil Robinson out of the tunnel with his hands cuffed behind his back, his own gun held to his head, and a vinyl sticker advertising Ethan's latest album slapped over his mouth.

Three down. Perfect. I'd brought duct tape from the car, so all we had to do was secure the prisoners, collect Trick and Vine, and then go home. If I drove fast enough, I could fit in a session on the firing range before dinner. Happy days.

"Pink, give Lili a minute to check the rest of the building, then bring Kelbyn to the platform."

Pink was one of Carmen's designated nicknames, and Lili was one of Ana's. We still had scarves over our faces, and I didn't want to identify ourselves. Why? Because there were plenty of other witnesses to the crime, and I had far better things to do with my time than sit for a police interview. We'd done our part. The hostages were safe if a little tearful, even Artemis and Isolde. I recognised them from the picture Mack had sent me. I very much suspected their next make-up tutorial would be on waterproof mascara.

Vine was sitting at the back, as Race had said, and yes, Trick was next to Isolde. Did he seriously like her? Trick had cleaned up well under Ethan's influence, but he still didn't strike me as the type who'd hook up with a Barbie doll. Artemis was sitting next to a guy as well. A boyfriend? Judging by the way she gripped his hand, the answer was in the affirmative. He was the oldest of the hostages, in his early twenties at a guess. The rest were teenagers.

Our next challenge would be getting Trick and Vine off the train. Presumably there was a button or a lever in the control booth, but could we release two people without setting the rest free as well? I didn't want seventeen former captives running around the sphere in the dark, and the police wouldn't appreciate having to round them up in the park later either. The monkeys and the capybaras were causing quite enough problems as it was.

Ana reappeared, and a tiny nod of her head told me the way was clear. A moment later, she crouched beside me and fished the duct tape out of my slimline backpack.

"Pink, okay to move." I raised an eyebrow at Ana. "A ball gag?"

"I thought it was yours."

"*Mine?*"

"I found it in the trunk of the Porsche. I wasn't going to say anything, but..."

"No, it's not fucking mine."

"Then whose...?"

Did my husband have a whole other dark side I was previously unaware of? No. No way. What about Carmen? Nate borrowed Black's car sometimes. Hmm... I couldn't see it. Dan wouldn't dare to take the Porsche for a spin, not after she'd managed to write off Black's Humvee a few years back. Who else? Ah... Sofia. She'd used it to drive to Virginia Beach with her boyfriend last month, and she *did* have a dark side.

"Fia," I mouthed, and Ana snorted.

Carmen appeared with Race in tow, and we arranged the three amigos face down on the platform. A whole roll of duct tape later, we had them trussed up like mummies, and I turned to face the people on the train. Apart from the occasional gasp and some sobs, they'd followed orders and stayed silent.

"Sorry about this interruption to your day, folks. We'll be leaving in a minute. Does anybody need medical attention?"

A few people mumbled "no," and the rest shook their heads.

"Great. We'll call the cops on our way out, and they'll be along shortly. All you have to do is tell them what happened."

Dan had been fumbling round in the control booth, and with a bit of guidance from Mack, she managed to release Trick's and Vine's restraints.

"Ready, guys?"

They didn't move. Why not?

One of the other riders came to life. "You can't do this!"

"You won't be here for long, and it's for your own safety."

"Let them go!" a girl yelled.

Huh? Let *them* go? Not *us*?

"She's gonna die," somebody else shouted.

The protests kept coming.

"Don't be so mean."

"Leave them alone."

"Go away."

Something hit me in the shoulder. I looked down

and saw a hair clip. Then a coin landed next to me, and a moment later, we were being pelted with everything from souvenir dinosaurs to cigarettes those kids should *not* have been smoking. Even a girl who'd obviously been crying threw a roll of Life Savers at me, and she looked *pissed*.

What the actual hell?

"Enough!" I bellowed. The throwing of projectiles ceased, probably because I was holding a gun. I pointed at Trick. "Explain. These men were threatening you, yes?"

"Yeah, but just before you showed up, the guy said he was only doing it so he could save his daughter. Like, he apologised."

He apologised? Gee, that was fine then.

"How does holding you hostage save his daughter? The first guy we caught said they wanted drugs."

One of the other kids spoke up. "Yeah, idiot. For his daughter."

The insult barely registered because suddenly I understood. *Sacker. Bio-D.* Ah, fuck. Had these fools kidnapped the two Sacker girls to force Pharma Daddy to hand over drugs his company made—probably for pennies—and sold at some exorbitant price? Big pharmaceutical companies could charge whatever they wanted, and people had no choice but to pay it.

I rolled Jeffrey over. "Is this true? You need drugs to save your sick daughter?"

He nodded, and I resisted the urge to facepalm. Instead, I unbuckled the ball gag.

"For the love of all that's holy, do you people not understand how ransom demands work? If you ask for a particular drug, then all the cops have to do is phone around the hospitals until they find whoever needed it, and then they'll track back and arrest you."

Jeffrey stared at me, unblinking. "I don't care. I'll go to jail if it saves my daughter. This is her last chance. The doctors said she'll die unless she gets treated in the next week. A cycle of Cytoblin costs five hundred thousand dollars, and she'll need two cycles at least."

"What does Cytoblin treat?"

"Acute lymphoblastic leukaemia."

"Hey, I saw something about that in my research," Mack told me. "A course of Cytoblin used to cost fifty thousand bucks, but Bio-D bought the patent and hiked the price tenfold."

Flaming Nora. What a bloody mess.

"You still can't go around..." I was about to say "waving guns at people," but then I realised I still had my Walther in my hand. Shit. I shoved it back into its holster. "Sick child or not, you can't just terrorise members of the public."

"I wouldn't have hurt anyone."

"He wouldn't," a kid called out. "He promised."

"My sister had cancer," a girl said. "It's horrible."

"What if he asked for money instead of the drugs?" another teenager suggested. "Then the cops couldn't find him."

I felt a headache coming on. "Hello? He held Sacker's daughters hostage."

"We won't tell anyone it was him," Isolde said. "Our dad's an asshole."

"We'll all say they weren't here," a boy with floppy hair offered. "Won't we?"

A chorus of yeses echoed back.

"They posted their whereabouts on fuckin'

Instagram," Dan pointed out. "The whole damn world knows they're here."

Ana started laughing. Sometimes, she had a really warped sense of humour.

"It's not bloody funny."

"*Da, eto tak*. It's hilarious."

"It is kind of funny," Carmen said. "You said today would be boring, and now the bad guys are the good guys, and the victim is practically a criminal, and there are monkeys everywhere."

Welcome to my life. MC Escher meets Hieronymus Bosch.

"What if I just give these people the money myself?" I suggested. "Then we can go back to the bar."

"Throw cash at the problem? Where's the fun in that?" Ana asked.

I leaned against a railing with my head in my hands. How could a straightforward rescue have gone so wrong? Much as I hated to admit it, the others had valid points, and I really couldn't stand David Sacker and his ilk. I was nobody's little fucking lady.

"Does anyone have family waiting for them outside?" I asked the teenagers. "People who'll start looking for you?"

One kid raised his hand. Guess the other parents all took the sensible option and stayed at home, which was where I'd be if Bradley hadn't been channelling Joseph Stalin.

"My parents are here, but I can text them," the kid said. "I'll tell them I went to see the dinosaurs. Bet my mom's in the bar, anyway."

I thought with fondness of the Steampunk Saloon, my cocktail sitting abandoned on the table. *Suck it up,*

Emmy.

Okay, what would I rather do? Save a girl's life while sticking it to Pharma Daddy, or send three desperate yet not particularly awful men to jail and have a bunch of youngsters hating my guts? Including Race, Trick, and Vine if their judgey expressions were anything to go by.

There wasn't really any contest, was there?

"Did you make any kind of contact with David Sacker?" I asked Jeffrey, just to check.

"Today? No. I wrote him begging for help a month ago, but he never wrote me back." Bastard. "Who *are* you people?"

"That doesn't matter." I let out a sigh. "All those in favour of stealing a million bucks from Mr. Sacker, raise your hands."

Every damn hand went up, including Artemis and Isolde Sackers'. Boy, their father really must be a piece of shit.

Could we do this?

I looked at my girls, and the crinkles around their eyes told me they were all grinning.

Yes, it seemed we fucking could.

CHAPTER 7

FIVE MINUTES LATER, everyone except Jeffrey Monteith sat around us on the platform. He still seemed kind of shell-shocked by developments, but I'd sent him into the control booth to monitor what was going on outside. His job now was to buy us time.

Kayleigh Monteith was being treated at Richmond General, and Mack had verified Jeffrey's story by calling Dr. Beech, our favourite ER doctor and a man who could easily be bought for donations to whatever charity project he happened to be running that month. After a promise from Blackwood to send a gift basket for his next fundraising raffle, he dug around in the computer system and found the information we needed. Kayleigh Monteith's situation was desperate. Her family had already sold everything they owned to fund medical expenses, and their insurance plan didn't cover a cutting-edge drug like Cytoblin.

It was her last chance.

Neil Robinson, it turned out, was her boyfriend. Kelbyn had shown us a photo of the three of them together in happier times. A pretty brunette standing between two grinning men, her arms around them both. Even though he was meant to be posing for the photographer, Neil's focus was on her, his smile for his girl rather than the camera. Young love. Once again, I was struck by the injustice in the world.

Now Neil huddled beside Kelbyn, hugging his knees to his chest and looking as if he might vomit at any given moment. Artemis didn't seem much better. She was nestled between the legs of the guy who'd been sitting next to her on the roller coaster, and he was doing his best to keep her calm. Isolde? She appeared a little more gung-ho. She'd already suggested increasing the ransom to five million bucks, one million for each time their father had told them that their new make-up business was a frivolous waste of their time. And that was just so far this week.

"We need a plan," I muttered. "I'm used to catching kidnappers, not being one."

"Simple," Carmen said. "Just think of every slip-up the *pendejos* you caught in the past made and avoid doing all of those things."

"Gee, why didn't I think of that?"

Okay, okay, I had to start at the beginning. We had two key objectives. One: get Pharma Daddy to cough up the cash, and two: make sure nobody in the sphere got caught.

To achieve the first, we'd need to go in fast and hard. No wiggle room allowed. And for the second, everybody needed to understand their role, remember their story, and agree to take the secret to the grave.

I addressed the last point first. Me and the girls still had scarves across our faces, but everyone had seen Race, Vine, and Trick. Probably knew their damn names too. I couldn't risk today's actions coming back to bite them on the ass later, nor did I want the Monteith family to get any nasty surprises a year or two into the future.

"Before we cross the line from morally dubious into abso-fucking-lutely illegal, everybody has to understand one thing. You. Cannot. Talk. About. This. To anyone. Not to your buddies on a drunken night out. Not to a girl you're trying to impress. Not to your parents or your siblings or your second cousin twice removed. After today, we'll be bound by a secret that could land us all in prison if the truth comes out. If anyone thinks they can't handle that, then now's the time to say so. It's not too late to call this off."

I gave them space to consider, no pun intended. The silence stretched into a full minute, and finally one guy near the back of the train spoke.

"If we can save a girl's life, then we should do it. Not to get kudos, but because it's the right thing to do."

"Drugs are too expensive," a girl said. "My brother's insulin costs six hundred bucks a month."

"President Harrison should fix that," somebody else chipped in. "Then we wouldn't have to turn vigilante."

President Harrison was trying, believe me. We'd had several conversations about it over the years, but first the right people had to get control of the senate, and that was a whole other story.

"Anybody want to back out? Speak now or forever hold your peace."

Nobody spoke. I took a careful look at Artemis, Isolde, and their friend. This would affect them more than anybody, and I crouched down so I could look them in the eyes.

"Are you okay with this? You'll have to lie, not just to your family but to the cops. We'll prepare you as best we can, but it won't be easy."

Artemis spoke up for the first time. "People look at

us and think we're spoiled. That we've only made it in the world because of who our father is. But we made it in spite of him. When we were kids, we used to pray together every night that God would send us new parents who loved us. Who cared enough to spend time with us. He didn't deliver."

"We've had five different moms, though," Isolde said. "Daddy's last Stepford Trophy Wife was shallower than a puddle of dog pee, and the current one won't say boo to a goose."

"Isolde!"

She shrugged. "Am I lying? Anyhow, we won't say anything. If you can get Daddy to part with his cash, you deserve a medal."

I always did like a challenge.

Plus I'd had a few sneak peeks into the minds of billionaires during my time. A million dollars might be a lot to a regular person, a life's work, but to the super-rich, it was just a really good party. A thousandth of their wealth. The equivalent of a hundred bucks, give or take, and most people would pay a hundred bucks if they thought it would ensure their family's safety. Even my darling husband might consider forking out the cash. Of course, he'd hunt the blackmailers down later and ensure they saw the error of their ways, but I was pretty sure Sacker wasn't a closet mercenary, so I wasn't too worried about the aftermath.

"And you?" I asked the guy next to Artemis. "How do you fit in?"

The three of them looked at each other, and again, Isolde answered. "Brett is Artemis's boyfriend. Except Daddy says he's a pleb, so Artemis had to hire him as our photographer just so she can spend time with him without getting yet another lecture."

Wow. The Sackers made my family look almost normal. And considering one of my three fathers was a genocidal maniac, another was a slightly offbeat drug lord, and my mother practically lived in rehab, that was saying something.

"Tell us what to do, and we'll do it," Artemis said, resigned. "We won't let a girl die."

CHAPTER 8

SO FAR, WE had Mack and Bradley on the outside. Jeffrey didn't have administrator access to the security camera system, but his boss did, and his boss kept the password written on a Post-it note stuck to the bottom of his computer screen. So now *we* had the password, and Mack had access to everything. She'd just raised an alarm for a leak over at the underwater exhibit, and now people were busy searching for that as well as the escaped animals. Bradley was watching the plaza plus keeping an eye on the kids. Mack checked in on the trio and reported that all was quiet outside and Josh and Tabby were chattering about shots and barrels, which meant they were either following in their mothers' footsteps or taking up drinking. I wasn't sure which was more concerning.

But we still needed somebody else. Somebody in New York to watch David Sacker. Somebody with the ethics of a sewer rat and an ability to blend in. I pulled out my phone.

"Hey, honey."

Fia groaned. "Uh-oh."

"You remember when my darling assistant called to invite you on a trip today, and you said you couldn't go because you'd booked a minibreak in New York? Was that true?"

"We got one of those last-minute deals. I was worried Bradley might check."

"Excellent. Can you do me a favour?"

"What kind of a favour? I've had no sleep. Some idiot crown prince in the hotel's presidential suite set off the fire alarm at three a.m. when he tried to roast a sheep in his bathtub."

"What the fuck?"

"Yeah, I know. And its buddy got loose in the hallway. Where would he even find a live sheep in New York?"

"Brooklyn."

"Seriously?"

"There's a poultry store. It sells goats too."

"How do you even know that?"

"I needed the sheep for an April Fool's joke. Don't worry—we found them good homes afterwards."

Dan chuckled in the background. "That was a great April Fool's joke."

My husband had been due to have a meeting in our Manhattan office with James Harrison—in his pre-presidency days, obviously, because the Secret Service would undoubtedly have confiscated the sheep otherwise—so Dan and I snuck in early, turfed the meeting room, and turned the flock loose. Of course, there were hiccups. One of those woolly bastards escaped out of the elevator and ran amok on the third floor, and even now, assholes still emailed me pictures of myself wrestling with it in the control room. Plus Dan had nearly died laughing and I'd had to pay the cleaners overtime because—newsflash—sheep pooped, but everyone agreed it had been a magnificent prank.

"I'm not even going to ask," Fia said.

"Better that you don't."

She sighed. "What is it that you want me to do?"

"Okay, so it's a long story, but we've sort of kidnapped two teenagers and now we need to get their father to pay a ransom. We want him to know we're keeping tabs on him."

"Wait, wait, wait. Isn't that exactly the opposite of your job?"

"On any other day, yes, but the kidnappees are on board with the plan, and their daddy's a greedy prick. We're thinking of this as doing our civic duty."

"I thought Bradley was making you go to an amusement park?"

"Yup, that's where we are. Except Bradley's stuck on the Ferris wheel because he inadvertently helped some monkeys make a break for freedom."

I heard a sleepy voice in the background. Leo, Fia's boyfriend.

"Who's that, gorgeous?"

"Just Emmy."

"Are we still going to MoMA today?"

"Later, but I need to pop out and help with a tiny bit of extortion first."

A pause. "Am I having a nightmare?"

"We all are, but don't worry; I'm sure it won't take long. Right?" Fia asked.

"Absolutely," I told her. "If he doesn't pay up before the park closes, we're fucked."

"Unlike me," she pointed out. "You owe Leo and me another dirty weekend."

"And I'll gladly send you anywhere you want. Now, here's what I need you to do... Mack's pinged David Sacker's phone, and he's—"

"David Sacker? The pharma guy?"

"You've heard of him?"

"We crossed paths at a party once. He was rude to a waitress, so I slipped a laxative into his drink. Does that mean you've got Artemis and Isolde there?"

While it didn't entirely surprise me that Fia had heard of David Sacker, I hadn't expected her to know who his kids were.

"You've met them too?"

"No, but I've started using Artis make-up when I go undercover at those fancy parties. Great colours, not tested on animals, recycled packaging. And my winged eyeliner was a mess until I followed one of Isolde's YouTube tutorials."

Hmm. My winged eyeliner looked as if a toddler had got loose with a Sharpie unless Bradley did it for me. Perhaps *I* should give those tutorials a try? But not right now, clearly. We had money to steal.

"Thanks for the tip. As I was saying, Mack's tracked Sacker's phone to his office building. If I text you the address, can you get over there and find me something I can use to prove we're watching him? Obviously I'll tell him not to call the cops or the FBI, but it'd be useful to know if they show up."

"On my way."

"Thanks, honey."

Fia blew me a kiss and hung up, and I moved to the next stage of the plan—receipt of the funds. Only an idiot would request a bag of cash in this day and age. There were so many things that could go wrong. Case in point: I'd been shot at during the purchase of a stolen painting years ago—essentially a ransom situation—and both the cash and the painting had vanished into the ether.

"Mack, can you set up an account to receive Bitcoin?"

I knew fuck all about cryptocurrencies other than they existed. And also that I'd accidentally become a crypto-millionaire because I went soft and let some cybergeek pay me for a job in Bitcoin back when they weren't worth much. I'd totally forgotten about it until I unearthed the password at the back of my desk drawer years later, and when I logged in to my account, I found out Bitcoin had soared in value.

But Mack, of course, knew everything.

"You don't want to use Bitcoin. Monero has a faster processing time and better anonymity."

"Can Sacker buy that with a credit card?"

"Sure, if he has a high enough limit."

He was a billionaire. Of course he had a high enough limit.

To make the ransom demand, I'd also need to use Mack's special phone app. Anyone trying to trace the call would get bounced around the world until they finished up at a banana stand in Sri Lanka. Or perhaps an internet café in Moscow. Or the Ryongsong Residence in Pyongyang. You get the idea. And we needed to come up with a solid enough story to keep the Monteiths out of the picture. If anyone realised Artemis and Isolde had been held inside the sphere, then the Monteiths' involvement would be all too evident.

That was Dan's area of expertise. She knew investigations, and her attention to detail was second to none. While I thought through what the hell I'd say to Sacker once Fia had confirmed she was in place, Dan arranged the kids into groups, then mapped out an alternative reality and gave each person a role in the fairy tale. One pair would claim they'd followed Artemis, Isolde, and Brett out of the sphere once the ride had finished. The two Sacker girls would sign old-fashioned autographs on theme park maps before they left, and the "witnesses" would of course have them as evidence.

Another pair would say they'd noticed the Sacker girls strolling across the plaza—at least, they thought so. They weren't quite sure, but after they'd checked on Instagram, they realised that yes, they'd been totally right.

Where was Brett during that time? In the bathroom. His story was that he'd been desperate for a pee for the last two rides, and he'd gone to answer the call of nature. On the way back to the plaza, he considered stopping to pick up cotton candy because Artemis had a sweet tooth, but the line was too long. Mack confirmed there was a ten-minute wait time. And when Brett came back, the girls had vanished. Once Mack finished disabling the security cameras, he'd head outside to start the ball rolling. Turned out that when he wasn't moonlighting as Artemis's photographer-slash-boyfriend, he was actually an actor, although he hadn't landed any big roles yet. Today, he had to put on the performance of his life.

Two other boys would say they'd seen the girls hurrying across the plaza with a man and a woman close behind. The boys wouldn't have a clue who Artemis and Isolde were until they saw news of the kidnapping on TV—because it surely would be on TV—and after they realised they had information, they'd do their civic duty and come forward. Had they unwittingly seen a crime in progress?

If they had, the malfeasance had nothing to do with the sphere. Neil and Kelbyn would swear blind the ride had been operating smoothly until suddenly, the lights went out. Bloody monkeys, blah, blah, blah.

We saved the most difficult roles for Trick, Vine, and Race. All three were accomplished bullshitters when the mood took them. They'd seen the girls and their abductors heading towards the east gate, which, according to Jeffrey, was the quietest. Plus the guy manning it right now was a slacker who didn't pay much attention to anything. Jeffrey had already given him two warnings, neither of which had had the slightest effect.

Mack got one of her sidekicks to mock up pictures of our two kidnapping suspects so everyone was on the same page with the descriptions, and we showed them to the audience on my phone.

"But don't be too accurate," Dan warned them. "That'll arouse more suspicions than if you don't remember a thing."

After retrieving Jeffrey's gun and magazine from beneath the track—we didn't want to leave those behind—Carmen helped Dan to put the kids under pressure, asking questions interview-style to find any weaknesses. And while they did that, Ana did what came naturally and scared the bejeebers out of Artemis and Isolde. They didn't need to fake their fear when I started recording them.

"Say your names, both of you," I snapped.

"I'm Artemis Sacker."

"Isolde S-S-Sacker."

"And what do you want to say to your father?"

Isolde burst into sobs, leaving Artemis to answer.

"Just give these people whatever they want. Please. *Please*."

Not bad. I turned the camera off. "The tears were a nice touch."

Isolde wiped her face with a sleeve. "I just thought of the time when I was six and I told Daddy I wanted to be an astronaut and he told me girls didn't become astronauts because our role in life was to grow up and find a good husband. And by good, he meant rich, because he wasn't going to support us forever. Talk about ruining a childhood dream. The first part, not the second part. As soon as I turn eighteen, Artemis and I are both moving far, far away from that walking mannequin of misogyny."

I gave her a tight smile. "Guess I'd better get ready to make this phone call."

Chapter 9

"WHAT'S HAPPENING?" I asked Fia half a second after my phone rang. This was taking too damn long. "Time's ticking."

I'd considered moving everyone out of the sphere, but I'd come to the conclusion it would cause more problems than it solved. We hadn't brought enough vehicles to get everyone off-site in one go, and a large group in the park would draw too much attention. If we split up, having pairs of teenagers wandering around loose would make it difficult to coordinate if we had to change the plan on the fly. No, the sphere was the best place for us to be right now, as long as we could keep any nosy maintenance people out. Thankfully, they were focused on the Ferris wheel, where Bradley reported a middle-aged lady had suffered a panic attack in the next capsule. He'd been helping her with breathing exercises through the glass. Jeffrey had admitted to stopping the wheel as a distraction—a simple software override—but after the monkeys got involved, it seemed that restarting it wasn't so straightforward. Thank goodness.

Brett was outside now, tentatively raising the alarm and establishing a false timeline. If the shit hit the fan and David Sacker did call the authorities, everyone would think the girls had been abducted at least half an hour before they actually left the park.

"Yeah, I know, I know. Sacker's on the move." Fia spoke quietly, and I could barely hear her above the noise of traffic, voices, and a siren wailing in the background. "He walked out of his building a minute after we arrived. There was a town car waiting."

"Shit."

"Don't worry—Leo and I hopped on a couple of Citi Bikes and followed. Hurrah for bad traffic. There's been a crash somewhere near Central Park."

"You took Leo with you?"

"I figured it'd be a good cover. He's better at surveillance now."

"I bloody hope so."

When Sofia first laid eyes on Leo, he'd been following one of her targets. She'd picked him out in about five seconds flat.

"Have faith, sister. Anyways, Sacker went into a townhouse on the Upper West Side. A blonde met him at the door, and according to Google, she's not the current Mrs. Sacker."

"A replacement?"

"Maybe. I mean, he stuck his tongue down her throat right on the doorstep, so..."

"Thanks, that's useful. Is there somewhere nearby you can watch from?"

"There's a café on the other side of the road. Leo's gone inside to order us coffee and croissants, and I'm gonna check the back of the building."

"Guess I'm ready to step over to the dark side."

"Good luck. I'll put breakfast on my expense account."

The moment of truth. Everything was in place. Now

it was my turn in the spotlight, and I couldn't afford to fuck this up. Of course, I'd give the Monteiths the money myself if it came to it, but that wouldn't teach David Sacker the lesson he so richly deserved.

I retreated to the passage and dialled. Artemis had given me her father's private number, so there was no secretary to pick up. Mack would run my voice through a scrambler, and the feed I got through my earpiece would let me hear what Sacker heard.

The phone rang. And rang, and rang, and rang. Tell me I wasn't going to bloody voicemail. I mean, should I leave a message?

"Yes?"

Thank fuck. Like every good CEO focused on making others' lives a misery, Sacker was a slave to his phone.

"We have your daughters."

Wow, I sounded like a robot in a straight-to-TV movie. At least there'd be no doubt that this wasn't a regular call.

"Who is this?"

Oh, please. "That doesn't matter. What matters is that unless you do exactly what we say, we'll kill them both."

"Is this a joke?"

"When I hang up, you'll receive an email with a video attachment. Then you'll know we're serious. The email will also contain the address of a Monero wallet." Plus a handy virus that would install onto his device when he opened the video, but of course I didn't mention that. "We want two million dollars by three o'clock. If you pay by two o'clock, the amount's reduced to one and a half million. Think of it as a prompt-payment discount. Miss the final deadline, and Artemis and Isolde will die. Tell anybody about this call, and they die. Call the police, they die. Leave your girlfriend's house, they die."

The sharp intake of breath told me I'd rattled him with that last sentence. Good. There were roughly two hours to go until the first deadline. Enough time for him to work out how to use cryptocurrency if he didn't already know, but not enough time for him or anyone else to stage an elaborate rescue. And now he knew we were watching.

"You're bluffing."

"Take a look at the video. Do you really want to be the man responsible for his daughters' deaths? You make a million bucks a week. We're talking ten days' earnings here. Are they not worth that much to you?"

"Now, listen to me..."

I hung up. There wasn't anything else to say, not at the moment, so I strode back to the platform. When all heads turned in my direction, I nodded once. It was done. Artemis stiffened for a second, then sagged sideways against her sister. Isolde just grinned. For sure I'd misjudged her initially—under the airbrushed make-up, she was a rebel, and I liked that.

"What do we do now?" Jeffrey asked.

"Now? We wait, and we hope Jimbo and his buddies keep your colleagues busy for long enough that they don't decide to take a closer look at the sphere."

At least we could take an educational tour of the universe in the meantime. I stared at a map of the Big Dipper for a moment, then began to pace.

CHAPTER 10

NOTHING HAPPENED FOR a full two minutes. That didn't surprise me. If I were Sacker, the first thing I'd do would be to phone Artemis and Isolde. Which would be pointless because their phones were turned off, but that'd take, say, thirty seconds each to get through to voicemail and leave his daughters messages. Perhaps he'd send a couple of texts as well? If he thought logically, he'd call Brett, who would tell him the girls were missing. Brett was also part of our early-warning system. If Sacker spoke to him, we'd get a clue where his head was at.

After questioning Brett, Sacker might need to throw on some clothes—depending on how far he'd got with his mistress—and then he'd check his email. Mack's bomb had landed in his inbox thirty seconds after I hung up—his private inbox, not his work one.

"Sacker's taken the bait," Mack told me. "He's on a Windows laptop. Just finding my way around now."

I lived my life firmly in the grey zone, that blurry line between black and white, between wrong and right. I didn't always abide by the law, but today, I'd wandered a little too close to the dark side for comfort. It left me twitchy. Perhaps it was fitting that this drama was unfolding in the gloom of the sphere? With just the emergency lighting on, the place looked more like a warehouse than outer space.

Isolde fell into step beside me. "Do you think Daddy will pay?" she asked.

"Honestly? I don't know."

"I don't think he will. He cares more about his bank balance than he does about us."

"Maybe he'll surprise you?"

Isolde made a face. "He doesn't do surprises. Order is the name of the game. If it's not on his calendar, it doesn't happen."

"We've got vision," Mack announced. "Check your phone. Still working on sound."

Without thinking, I swiped up and was greeted by the sight of David Sacker in a hastily tied silk robe, seated in front of his laptop at what appeared to be a dressing table judging by the bottles of perfume and moisturiser at the edges of the picture. Mack had taken over his webcam. Which on any other job would have been great, but he wasn't alone. A half-naked blonde was leaning over his shoulder, her long hair brushing the keys. And of course, Isolde saw her.

"Ah, shit," I muttered. "Sorry."

She just shrugged. "Like I said, he's ruled by his schedule. We're due a new stepmom. It's been two years since he married the last one."

"You're not upset?"

"Not really. They're basically interchangeable. The only problem is keeping up with the names. Hey, Artemis—we're getting a new stepmom."

Artemis groaned. "Another one?"

"Sure looks that way, although you can hardly tell the difference between her and Shandi."

"Shandi? He's married to Carissa at the moment."

Isolde rolled her eyes. "Right. Carissa. I bet the new one's twenty-five. They're always twenty-five. In ten years, he'll be scouting our friends for hook-ups."

"Can you just stop talking?" Artemis asked.

"Why? It's the truth."

Mack spoke up again. "Sacker just googled 'What is a Monero?'"

"That's got to be a good sign, right?"

Last month, Bradley had read a book on Chinese spirituality, and before he even finished the first chapter, he'd been gushing about cosmic duality and feng shui. In between rearranging my furniture and planting a six-foot-high statue of Buddha next to the helipad, he'd lectured me on the concept of yin and yang—the belief that two sets of opposing yet complementary energies govern the universe. Dark and light. Sun and moon. Male and female.

Negative and positive.

After today, I was starting to believe in it because as soon as we got one tiny bit of good news, the bad news followed.

"Uh-oh," Mack said.

"What?"

"They just caught Jimbo."

Ah, crap. Our unwitting partner in crime would soon be back in monkey jail. And it was harder for us to follow the goings-on in the park now because Mack had shut down most of the cameras.

"We oughta create a website called 'What is a Monero?' with really, really simple instructions."

"I could get Agatha to do it, but Sacker's a CEO. Surely he should be able to follow one of the basic how-to pages that's already out there?"

Yeah, so CEOs weren't necessarily smart. I'd found that out through years of experience. Case in point: Sacker still hadn't called Brett.

"Possibly."

"I'll get Agatha to write out instructions just in case. If he looks like he's having trouble, we can email them."

This was the part of the job I hated the most. The waiting. Where events were out of my control and there was little I could do to alter the outcome. Isolde headed back to her sister and they set about changing their appearances for the trek across the park. Dan and Carmen were still drilling the kids through their stories, and I caught Ana's eye. Nodded towards the wormhole. While she checked the route to the main door again, I headed back the way we'd come in.

In the background, Mack was grumbling about obsolete drivers for the microphone, and should she risk installing updated ones? Perhaps if she made a pop-up box that said it was an automatic update, Sacker wouldn't get suspicious. Then the blonde said something, flipped her hair, and flounced across the bedroom. Sacker went after her.

"How long will installing an updated driver take?" I asked Mack.

"A minute or so."

"Do it."

The passage to the fire exit was clear, and by the time I got back to the platform, Sacker was still pacing the townhouse bedroom, the blonde trailing behind him like a forlorn puppy.

"The Ferris wheel's turning again," Mack said.

"Send Bradley back to the car when he gets down. We'll want to make a swift departure."

"Sure, I'll do that. And we should have sound... now."

A pause, and then the blonde's voice reached my ears. Ouch. If it got much higher in pitch, the neighbourhood dogs would come running.

"It's probably a stunt," she said. "For YouTube or something. Come back to bed, baby."

"We don't know that for sure."

Sacker scrubbed a hand through his hair, leaving it skew-whiff. Getting a little stressed? Well, so was I, because if they treated this as a joke, then the Monteiths wouldn't get their money. What was wrong with Sacker? Was he really blind enough to his daughters' personalities that he thought they'd be capable of playing such a sick prank? Granted, the "abduction" wasn't entirely above board, but it was far from a social media scam. I'd met the girls less than an hour ago and I already knew they had neither the audacity nor the need to trick their father like that.

"They're attention-seeking. Remember last month when Artemis interrupted dinner with some question about school?"

"That was kind of a big deal, Chantelle. She was thinking of changing her major from politics to videography."

"There you go—*videography*." Chantelle waved a hand towards the laptop. "See? It's just another project for her."

"Neither of the girls was holding that camera."

"So? It was probably that hanger-on Artemis hired. What a waste of money! He got the lighting totally wrong. Everyone knows you should use a ring light for close-ups."

Ugh. The woman was just awful.

"You're right! What's his name?" Sacker snatched up his phone and began scrolling. "Brent? Trent?"

"Brett?"

Sacker found the number, dialled, and switched the phone onto speaker while it rang. Meanwhile, Chantelle had a brainwave. Must have fried every tiny fucking cell in her skull in the process, but she picked up her own phone and checked Instagram.

"He's with them today." She waved her mobile triumphantly. "Told you."

Brett answered. "Hello?"

"It's David Sacker... Artemis and Isolde's father. Are they with you?"

"They were, but I can't find them. Like, they disappeared right in the middle of SciPark, and now their phones are turned off. Why? Did they call you?"

"What do you mean, they disappeared?"

"I went to take a leak, and they were sitting in the shade checking Insta, and when I came back, they weren't there anymore. So I figured they'd gone to the car to get a charger or something, but that was nearly an hour ago, and the charger's still in the car and no one remembers seeing them. Man, this whole place is in chaos—a bunch of monkeys got out. A couple of the rides broke down too. Maybe the girls got caught up in the crowds? Want me to get Artemis to call you when I find them?"

"I already got a call," Sacker said. His voice had dropped to a strangled whisper, a far cry from the "I'm right, you're wrong" tone he customarily used.

"That's great—what did they say?"

A commotion at the other end of the platform

caught my eye. Jeffrey Monteith was on the phone, and he didn't seem happy. Dan was there in a second, first listening and then gesturing. A pep talk by the look of things.

David Sacker didn't have that support. He'd deflated onto a tackily ornate chair in front of the dressing table while Chantelle pouted behind him, and he was most definitely out of his element. This was one situation he couldn't order and argue his way out of.

"The call wasn't from the girls," he told Brett. "They appear to have been abducted."

"What?" A long pause. "If that's a joke, it's not funny."

"You think I'd joke about something like that?" Sacker snapped.

"N-n-no, sir. They've been *kidnapped*?" That was a nice note of fear in Brett's voice. "Have you called the cops? I should tell park security. There're cameras and —"

"No! The person who called said...they said not to contact the police."

"So what the hell do we do?"

"They want a ransom."

"You're gonna pay it?"

"I don't know. I just don't—"

"Out now!" Dan directed.

Fuck. "What's happening?"

"The maintenance crew's coming in. Jeffrey tried to stop them, but the park director overruled him."

Okay, we'd planned for this. While the crew came in through the main entrance, we'd retreat to the vestibule by the emergency exit, then leave in small groups. Except...

"Slight hitch," Mack said.

Don't tell me problems, tell me solutions. "What hitch?"

"I left the camera pointing at the fire door turned on so I could monitor any movements, and a group of park rangers is standing right next to it, chatting."

And then from Bradley, "Hey, it's me. What'd I miss?"

CHAPTER 11

FORGET MY EARLIER comment. The waiting wasn't the worst part of a job. No, the point when everything went wrong at the same time, that was the worst part.

"Sorry, sorry, he just helped himself to an earpiece," Mack said.

"Bradley, go back to the car. We're dealing with a situation."

"What situation? Can I help? I'm excellent at helping."

"Sure, you can help. Just go ask the staff hanging out behind the sphere if they'd mind fucking off because we're all about to get caught."

And then it got even worse. We were moving along the passage now, feeling our way in the near-darkness, when Artemis glanced across at my lit phone. She'd lost the make-up and tucked her hair under a borrowed ball cap, but unfortunately, she was still pretty enough to draw attention.

"Oh, no. No way. Not her."

"What? Who?"

She jabbed at the screen with one manicured nail. "Is *that* my dad's new girlfriend?"

I was desperately trying to keep track of all the threads. Sacker had told Brett to stay put exactly where he was and hung up, and Chantelle was back to her conspiracy theories. They should play the girls at their own game, she suggested. Call their bluff and get the police involved—that would teach them not to waste everyone's time. Or perhaps she, Chantelle, could post a video on social media letting the world know how inconsiderate the girls were being?

"You know her?"

"I think so. She's a temp in his office, and also a two-faced bitch."

"Why do you say that?"

"Because I had to deliver some papers for Daddy one day, and while I was there, she asked to model for one of our Artis videos, and when I said no, she said she totally understood and then bad-mouthed me to some other lady in the bathroom."

"You overheard her?"

Artemis nodded. "Once you hear her voice, you never get it out of your head." Tell me about it. I'd need to drill out my ear canals when I got home. "She'll do anything for publicity. I checked out her Insta, and it's basically just her posing in skimpy outfits plus doing promos for the brands everyone else turns down."

The kid in front of me tripped on the stairs, and I shot out a hand to grab his sweater while I watched the unfolding scene in Sacker's townhouse. It had morphed into a full-on domestic, and if there was one thing worse than Chantelle talking, it was Chantelle yelling. I wanted to rip out my earpiece and stomp on it.

"*You* were the one who said nobody gets rich by giving money away to other people," she accused.

"I was talking about competitors, not a fucking kidnapper."

"And I keep telling you, there *is* no kidnapper.

They're just acting out."

"My daughters wouldn't do that."

Chantelle snorted. "Like you'd know. You don't spend any time with them. Trust me, I'm a woman and I know how they think—it's a trick."

"Get out."

"Huh?"

"I can't think with you screeching at me. Just get out."

"But I live here."

"Not anymore."

Chantelle's jaw dropped as Sacker yanked open the bedroom door and then pushed her through it. On the surface, that seemed like a good move, but warning bells began ringing in my head. *She'll do anything for publicity. It's a stunt. I know how women think.* Left to her own devices, Chantelle was likely to do something monumentally stupid, and Sacker hadn't paid the ransom yet.

"Mack, find us a way out of here."

"Give me two minutes. I'm trying to shut down the power to that giant human body."

"We don't have two minutes," I hissed.

I could already hear voices on the platform. Jeffrey, Kelbyn, and Neil would try to occupy the newcomers, but if they decided to take a look at that electrical cabinet in the rear vestibule...

"Never fear, Bradley's here."

What the actual fuck?

"Bradley, what are you doing?"

"Leave it to me."

"Mack, what's he doing?"

"I don't freaking know!"

"Bradley—"

A scream came from outside. A child's scream, and I saw Ana's silhouette stiffen in front of me. Shit, was that Tabby? A mother knew, right? A second scream came, a boy's this time, followed by a third that was one hundred percent Bradley's, and then the shouting started.

"Snake!"

"Snake!"

"Snake!"

I heard footsteps running across the plaza outside, going away from the sphere, thank goodness. More screams, other people's this time.

"What snake?" a guy asked.

"A big one," Josh told him. "Huge. Like the one that ate the guy in *Snakes on a Plane*."

"A Burmese python?"

Nice job, kid. There was one of those in the rainforest exhibit, and earlier when I'd looked into its habitat, it had been barely visible behind a moss-covered tree stump. Somebody would have to go over to the giant glasshouse to check whether it had escaped or not, which would give us enough time to get the hell out of the park.

But Carmen still wasn't happy. "Who let Josh watch that movie? He's only seven years old."

Er...

"Can we talk about that later?"

"Emmy!"

"The rangers have moved away," Mack said. "I've shut off the camera."

"Take your group and go," I told Carmen. "Go!"

I felt rather than saw her dirty look as she slipped

out the door with her four assigned kids. The plan called for me to go third, but I gave Dan a nudge.

"Swap places? I've got a horrible feeling the shit's about to hit the fan in New York, and I need to call Fia."

"Understood."

In the accomplice lottery, I'd drawn Artemis, two boys, and another girl. The kids had been prepped well. The older of the boys held Artemis's hand as we strolled across the plaza, and I caught a flash of turquoise in the distance ahead of us. Bradley was on his way to the car too. Phew. I couldn't take any more drama today. Dan had Isolde, her three boys would come afterwards on their own, and Ana would wait to buy her team snacks from the kiosk and then they'd bring up the rear. Not a care in the fucking world.

"Fia?"

"What's up?"

"The blonde's gonna be leaving the townhouse imminently, and you need to keep her occupied."

"Uh, wait one second, caller."

Shit, Chantelle had left already? The screech of chair legs on a wooden floor followed by a door opening and then the *slap, slap, slap* of feet on paving slabs told me Fia was on her way along the street.

"What's happening?" Artemis whispered. "Will our dad pay?"

"Shh."

I needed to hear Fia. Judging by the muted city sounds, she'd put her phone in her pocket while she hunted down Chantelle. Plus I had to stay aware of what was going on around us. The staff were understandably edgy after today's events, and all it would take was one misplaced glance... A teenager in a ranger's uniform veered in our direction, and I instructed everyone to head left between a fake cowboy saloon and a virtual-reality bucking-bronco ride. We could go out of our backup exit and circle back to the car.

"Hey!" Chantelle complained in my ear. "You just broke my phone."

"Oh, I'm so sorry. Here, let me see."

"Ow! What the...you..."

Did I mention that Fia carried knockout drugs the way most women carried tampons? You know, for those little emergencies. I heard muffled fumbling for a few moments, and then a man spoke, a stranger.

"Is she okay?"

"Bad break-up," Fia said, apologetic. "She fell off the wagon again. Don't worry, sweetie, we'll get you home."

"Y-y-you monshter."

"Sorry, she really doesn't like men right now, and you've got the same colour hair as her ex, so..."

"I get it, I get it." The man's voice faded. "Hope she sobers up soon."

Chantelle would wake up in an alley somewhere, or maybe on a park bench if she was lucky. Fia would stick around long enough to make sure the whining bitch didn't get mugged, then she'd vanish back into the city crowds. I owed her one hell of a vacation for that little favour.

"Sacker's setting up a Monero address," Mack said. "We did it, guys. I'm gonna pack up and head in your direction. Agatha can keep monitoring progress from headquarters."

I knew then that things would be okay. Our

cobbled-together team had beaten the odds and won. Kayleigh Monteith was going to get the treatment she needed, and there was one more unexpected bonus—I very much doubted Chantelle would become stepmom number six. But if Bradley thought I was ever going to another "amusement" park, he had another think coming.

Next time, I'd stay at home and learn to crochet instead.

CHAPTER 12

YOU REMEMBER I said I knew things would be okay? Well, I might have been a teensy bit premature with that assumption. When I got back to the vehicles with Artemis, Bradley was unlocking the doors of Black's Porsche, because of course he'd got himself a spare key from somewhere.

On any other day, I'd have congratulated him on his efforts with the non-snake, reminded him to be damn careful if he drove Black's car anywhere—he'd knocked a wing mirror off Black's last SUV because he decided to check his hair in the mirror while backing it out of the garage—and settled Artemis into the car. But all those thoughts quickly became redundant when I saw Josh and Tabby. Fuuuuuck. I scrabbled for my phone.

"Dan, new plan. I'm going to drive Bradley and the littlies far, far away while you tell Carmen and Ana there was an emergency."

"What emergency? I had to circle around the runaway mine train and they got ahead of me. They'll hit the parking lot any second."

The prickling hairs on the back of my neck told me she was right.

"Too late," I whispered as Ana glided to a halt next to me.

"Why does my daughter look like a baby hooker?"

Carmen was right behind her. "And why does my son look like a drag queen?"

The more pertinent question: why in the name of fuck hadn't Mack warned me? With advance notice, I could have prevented a murder. Tabby was wearing pink vinyl hot pants and a vest top, both decorated with tattered chiffon. Personally, I thought she looked more like a belly dancer than a hooker, but potayto, potahto. Josh was channelling a Disney Princess crossed with Betty Rubble in a dinosaur-skin dress. Both kids had false eyelashes, glittery hair, and what seemed to be an entire cosmetic range trowelled onto their faces.

"You told me to keep them occupied," Bradley said to Ana, hands on his hips. "Like, you literally said I should use my imagination and stop them from getting bored until the wheel started working again."

"I meant draw a picture or something, not this." She took a step forward, and Bradley took a step back, right onto my foot. "Where the hell did those shorts come from?"

"The gift store. They started off as a tote bag, but I had a pair of scissors and a sewing kit in my purse."

Bradley's purse was a fucking Tardis.

"Where are Josh's pants?" Carmen asked.

"I upcycled them into his belt and Tabby's vest."

So Josh was stuck in the dress until he got home? I quickly turned my laugh into a cough and hoped Nate would see the funny side when that glitter dropped all over the carpet.

"Guys, we need to go. Bradley, you can ride with Dan, okay?"

"But I don't want to die."

"I hate to break this to you, but you're going to die

whichever car you go in. Carmen, you'll need to take Tabby because if those sparkles get on Artemis and Isolde, the cops are going to ask questions about where they've been." Plus Black definitely wouldn't see the funny side if his car ended up all sparkly. "Let's go."

Ana pointed at the baby seat just as Mack staggered up with her electronic shit and Bradley's shopping.

"Okay, fine. Let's move that abomination into Carmen's car, and then we can go."

I'd think of some other punishment for Black.

Sacker paid the million-and-a-half bucks with two minutes to spare. Once Mack had confirmed receipt and moved the money out of reach, we said our goodbyes to Artemis and Isolde. They weren't bad kids underneath all the warpaint. Turned out it was their father's fault that they'd started their make-up empire. The succession of stepmothers he'd brought into their lives specialised in the superficial, and although the women had shirked their responsibilities when it came to emotional support, they *had* taught the sisters every tip and trick on how to make themselves look pretty. Now the girls were sharing that knowledge with the world and making money out of it. Stepmom number five, Carissa, had been relatively supportive when it came to setting up Artis—apparently she'd finished her MBA before she worked out that getting a sugar daddy was more lucrative than getting a job. Artemis admitted that she actually quite liked Carissa, but what was the point in getting close to a stepmom when they'd be gone in a year or two? My heart hurt for both daughters. Two princesses trapped in an ivory tower.

We dropped them half a mile from a gas station, out of sight of any cameras or passing vehicles. Artemis would wait five minutes and then call Brett, who in turn would call Sacker with the good news of their release.

Both girls hugged me, and Ana too although not quite so tightly.

"Don't be a stranger," I murmured to Artemis.

"I won't. Does it sound crazy to say this turned out to be a good day?"

"Yes, but we're all crazy here, so you fit in quite well."

Isolde gave me a shy smile. "Do you think Trick might want to go on a date with me someday?"

"Ask him. You'll like the answer. But leave it a few weeks first, yeah?"

She nodded, and her smile turned into a grin. "See you soon."

EPILOGUE

THE POLICE INVESTIGATION went nowhere. What did go somewhere? The chat group the "hostages" formed following their "ordeal." In the sphere, they'd said they wanted to stay in touch, so Mack set up the app for them and Dan organised the invitations, although Artemis and Isolde didn't receive theirs until after the case had gone cold.

Three months on, and I was oddly proud of everything we'd achieved on that day. Those teenagers came from different backgrounds, different social classes, even different countries, yet they were constantly building each other up. Anonymity had fallen by the wayside, and Dan was a member of the group too, just to keep an eye on things. Every day the kids helped each other with everything from homework to fashion advice to relationship woes, if going out for burgers counted as a relationship. Dan gave me regular updates, usually while we were waiting for our morning caffeine to kick in.

But the best part? Kayleigh Monteith's cancer was in partial remission. The Cytoblin had worked its very expensive magic and kicked the cancer cells' ass. Would it last? The doctors couldn't say, but they were hopeful.

Bradley's not-so-dulcet tones sounded from the hallway, then the front door slammed, and more voices headed in my direction—Dan, Trick, Vine, Race, Brett, Artemis, and Isolde. They'd all be staying at Riverley this weekend since the home Dan shared with Ethan only had two spare bedrooms. Black and I would decamp next door to Little Riverley because while I didn't mind kids quite as much as I used to—as long as they came in small doses—I still valued my sleep. The group obviously couldn't tell the truth about how they'd crossed paths, so they'd all arranged to be at the same pop concert a month after the SciPark incident, and that was where they'd officially met. I'd had to speak to David Sacker to set up today's trip, and he'd called me by my actual name this time. Progress.

"Wait a second." I grabbed Dan as she walked past me and flicked a piece of glitter out of her hair. "Okay, you're good to go."

"That damn stuff. I've had the car detailed nine times, and it's still lurking in the cracks. I even had the floor mats changed."

"Don't worry, honey. You're due a prang anytime now, so you'll have a great excuse to replace the whole vehicle."

"Never before have I hoped to hear the sound of crunching metal."

Carmen had also suffered from the abundance of glitter, but after Nate borrowed her G-Wagen and turned up for a management meeting looking like Tinker Bell, he drove straight to the dealership and traded it in for a new one. Bradley was banned from going anywhere near it.

Speaking of Bradley, he'd given up on the rainforest idea. That should have been good news except he'd been up late watching National Geographic and now he had his heart set on meerkats, together with a desert vista for them to live in. Oh, and he wanted a full-sized Ferris wheel too. I'd been forced to ship him off to Milan in the hope that the boutiques would distract him for long enough to forget those ideas, and boy was my credit card taking a hammering. But the pain was worth it. Meerkats might have been cute to look at, but I'd done a little research and come to the conclusion that they were much better off living in Botswana than in my backyard. All I truly wanted was a hammock plus a gin and tonic.

"How's it going?" I asked Artemis once the others had said their hellos and disappeared off to the swimming pool. She'd always been the most reserved of the group, but today, she seemed different. More relaxed, not quite so robotic. I hadn't seen her in person since that day at SciPark, but sometimes I watched her YouTube videos. Still fucked up my eyeliner every time, though.

"Good. Like, really good."

"Dan said your dad is easier to live with now?"

"The kidnapping totally unnerved him."

"I bet."

"Last week, he said it was an expensive lesson, but one he needed to be taught. That he'd had his priorities wrong his whole life. His dad taught him that success was measured by appearance, by shows of wealth and the number of zeroes on his bank balance, and he'd been so busy focusing on earning more, more, more that he'd forgotten to take care of the things that were important."

"So he's changed?"

"Sort of. I mean, he's trying. Like, he stays home at

least two evenings a week plus one weekend day now. We even eat dinner together. Plus he wants us to go on vacation, the whole family, and Carissa's freaking out because she signed up to be a trophy wife and now she has to spend two weeks in the Caribbean talking to a man she barely knows."

"But she's talking to you."

Artemis nodded. "She's only seven years older than me, and she was really worried after the kidnapping. Kept asking if we were okay and if there was anything she could do to help. I hope Daddy doesn't ditch her."

"Look on the bright side—at least he doesn't have Chantelle waiting in the wings anymore."

On the day of the kidnapping, Fia had emptied a miniature of whisky down Chantelle's top, then propped her up outside a soup kitchen and waited until a kind-hearted soul dragged her inside. Last we heard, she was working as an assistant weather girl for some obscure TV station in Iowa.

"Oh, that would've been a disaster. And even if Daddy does get another divorce, I think Carissa and I will still be friends. She's helping with Artis. I'd offer her a job at the company. Did Bradley get those samples we sent? The new mascara?"

"You're talking to the wrong person, I'm afraid. I basically wear whatever he puts on my face, and I don't pay any attention to the labels. No offence."

"I bet you think we're really shallow, huh?"

"Honestly? I did at first, but I don't anymore. You help women to feel good about themselves, and that's admirable."

"Did Bradley mention our new project?" Probably, but I doubt I'd been listening. "It's called 'Artis Gives

Back.' We've just launched a range of false lashes and eyebrows designed especially for people fighting cancer. Plus we're selling an exclusive high-gloss moisturising lipstick, and we're using the profits from that to pay off lunch debt one school at a time. Daddy even offered to match the amounts, and Isolde asked if he was feeling okay. I think that was another blow for him."

Sad. Not that Isolde had hit him with the truth, but that it had taken so long for him to see it.

"That's not necessarily a bad thing."

"I just wish he'd been like this our whole lives, you know? Think of all the good he could have done. We suggested he set up a hardship program for specialist drugs, and he agreed, but if he'd done that years ago..."

"You can't change the past, only the future. Baby steps." David Sacker still had to work on the price-gouging, but I'd heard on the grapevine that he'd implemented an employee welfare program at Bio-D. "How are you holding up after what happened?"

Yes, the second part of the "kidnapping" had been a total fabrication, but the initial hostage situation in the sphere had been all too real. And the girls had few people they could talk to about it.

"Okay, I guess. I haven't been to the movies since that day. The thought of walking into a dark, enclosed space makes me nervous."

"We've got a movie theatre here. No monkeys, no roller-coaster train, and no gun-toting maniacs." Ana had gone out for the day. "Have at it."

Artemis smiled a rare genuine smile. "Being held hostage was scary, but also the best thing that ever happened to me."

"Just try not to do it again, okay?"

She giggled. "I promise. Are you coming swimming?"

"Not today." Today, I had to speak to a man about an arson attack. "Have fun."

WHAT'S NEXT?

The next book in the Blackwood Security series is *The Scarlet Affair*...

The Scarlet Affair

Eight dead men. Eight grieving widows...

After a series of particularly nasty home invasions, Blackwood Security is hired to catch the killers. With the company's reputation at stake, everyone on the team is desperate to solve the mystery, unaware that there's a traitor in their midst.

Cade Duchamp's eager to help, but a minor indiscretion with the wrong girl leaves him banished to undercover duty. He's always liked motorbikes, but he doesn't like being a biker. Uncomfortable leather, an itchy beard, a lack of soap—need he say more? Cade wants to be back at head office, hunting down the real bad guys. At least, he does until five-year-old Scarlet turns up. The daughter he never knew he had.

Taylor Hancock likes to fade into the background. As an office cleaner, she can come to work, do her job, and avoid those dreaded social interactions. But nobody says no to Emmy Black, and as Scarlet's new nanny, Taylor's forced way out of her comfort zone into a world of shopping trips, parties, and playdates.

The only problem?
She's the traitor.

Find out more here: www.elise-noble.com/scarlet

My next book will be *The Girl with the Emerald Ring*, the twelfth book in the Blackwood Security series...

The Girl with the Emerald Ring

After a nasty divorce, Bethany Stafford-Lyons is forced to transform herself from a high-society housewife into one of London's worker bees. Using a last connection to her previous life, she lands a job at Pemberton Fine Arts, a world-renowned gallery and restoration studio. With her art degree, it should have been the perfect role, but she soon finds interning for Hugo Pemberton is a challenge in more ways than one.

Eight years ago, Alaric McLain got fired from the FBI after an undercover operation ended in disaster. Still missing? One masterpiece, ten million dollars in cash and diamonds, and his once-glowing reputation. When he retreated overseas to lick his wounds, he made a vow—he'd find The Girl with the Emerald Ring if it was the last thing he did.

The trail leads to Chelsea, where assisted by his ex-girlfriend and a seventeen-year-old brat he wants to handcuff to a railroad track, Alaric's soon embroiled in a game of cat and mouse with a talented team of thieves. Let the fun begin...

For more details: www.elise-noble.com/emerald

If you enjoyed Sphere, please consider leaving a review.

For an author, every review is incredibly important. Not only do they make us feel warm and fuzzy inside, readers consider them when making their decision whether or not to buy a book. Even a line saying you enjoyed the book or what your favourite part was helps a lot.

WANT TO STALK ME?

For updates on my new releases, giveaways, and other random stuff, you can sign up for my newsletter on my website:
www.elise-noble.com

Facebook:
www.facebook.com/EliseNobleAuthor

Twitter: @EliseANoble

Instagram: @elise_noble

If you're on Facebook, you may also like to join Team Blackwood for exclusive giveaways, sneak previews, and book-related chat. Be the first to find out about new stories, and you might even see your name or one of your ideas make it into print!

And if you'd like to read my books for FREE, you can also find details of how to join my advance review team.

Would you like to join Team Blackwood?

www.elise-noble.com/team-blackwood

END OF BOOK STUFF

Back before I started writing, when I actually had free time, I had a season ticket to Thorpe Park, which is a big amusement park in the south of England. I don't live too far away from there, so I could shoot over in the summer evenings when they were open late and miss all the crowds.

One of my favourite rides was an indoor rollercoaster called X:/No Way Out, set in a giant black pyramid. You rode backwards in the dark. Even the queue was fun, winding through a series of computer-virus-themed rooms with lights and lasers and all that shizzle.

And then there was Vortex, a giant rotating pendulum that strapped you in so tight you could hardly move before whirling you in circles.

Thorpe Park also had a little farm back then. You rode there on a train or a boat, and you could feed the animals and whatnot. Sadly, the farm is long gone and X has been overhauled and turned into a Walking Dead ride (an idea for another book, perhaps?). Vortex is still going, though :)

Anyhow, I thought I'd take a trip down memory lane and mash the whole lot together, and that turned into Sphere. At first, it was going to be a straight hostage situation, but then I figured it would be a lot more fun to turn the bad guys into the good guys and the good guys into the bad guys and give Emmy a nice little moral dilemma too. I hope you enjoyed the ride.

Next up is Alaric's story. The reason it's taken so long for another book in the Blackwood Security series to come out is because one book turned into three books with interlinked storylines, kind of like the original Black trilogy. Which meant I wanted to write them all before I published the first so I could avoid any continuity-related fuck-ups. Plus they're really long, lol. So, what does that mean? It means that *The Girl with the Emerald Ring* will be out at the end of August, and Blackwood Security books thirteen and fourteen (*Red After Dark* and *When the Shadows Fall*) are already written to follow on after that. They just need editing. And while that's happening, I'm writing the fifth instalment of the Electi series ready for next year!

As always, I couldn't have published this book without help from my awesome team. Huge thanks to Jeff, Renata, Terri, Musi, David, Stacia, Jessica, Nikita, Quenby, Jody, and Sandra for beta reading; Nikki for editing; and John, Debi, and Lizbeth for proof reading :)

And also thank you to you, the reader, for your support!

Elise

OTHER BOOKS BY ELISE NOBLE

The Blackwood Security Series
For the Love of Animals (Nate & Carmen - prequel)
Black is my Heart (Diamond & Snow - prequel)
Pitch Black
Into the Black
Forever Black
Gold Rush
Gray is my Heart
Neon (novella)
Out of the Blue
Ultraviolet
Glitter (novella)
Red Alert
White Hot
Sphere (novella)
The Scarlet Affair
Spirit (novella) (TBA)
Quicksilver
The Girl with the Emerald Ring (2020)
Red After Dark (2020)
When the Shadows Fall (TBA)

The Blackwood Elements Series
Oxygen
Lithium

Carbon
Rhodium
Platinum
Lead
Copper
Bronze
Nickel
Hydrogen (TBA)

The Blackwood UK Series
Joker in the Pack
Cherry on Top (novella)
Roses are Dead
Shallow Graves
Indigo Rain
Pass the Parcel (TBA)

Blackwood Casefiles
Stolen Hearts

Blackstone House
Hard Lines (TBA)
Hard Tide (TBA)

The Electi Series
Cursed
Spooked
Possessed
Demented
Judged (TBA)

The Trouble Series
Trouble in Paradise

Nothing but Trouble
24 Hours of Trouble

Standalone
Life
Coco du Ciel (TBA)
Twisted (short stories)
A Very Happy Christmas (novella)

Books with clean versions available (no swearing and no on-the-page sex)
Pitch Black
Into the Black
Forever Black
Gold Rush
Gray is my Heart

Audiobooks
Pitch Black
Into the Black
Forever Black